Dancing Skies & City Lights

SHELEILA D'PAIVA

Typeset in Adobe Garamond Pro 12/17pt

 A catalogue record for this work is available from the National Library of Australia

NATIONAL LIBRARY OF AUSTRALIA

National Library of Australia Catalogue-in-Publication data:
Dancing Skies and City Lights/Sheleila D'Pava

ISBN: 978-0-6456259-6-7
(Paperback)

ISBN: 978-0-6456259-7-4
(Ebook)

To all the wondrous souls, stay curious xoxo

1

Life

I could hear someone faintly calling my name in the distance. The foot-steps were getting closer, I snapped out of the daydream and started to refocus my eyes.

'Kate? Kate? Do you have that Balentine presentation ready for me?'

There was a sense of urgency in my manager's voice from down the corridor, and I was forced back into reality. Work. I was at work. It was another day. Another meaningless day in this cramped, sterile office. Another day in this rat-race. I swivelled my ergonomic office chair around to the part of my desk that was almost facing the window. *This will wake me up,* I hoped, the sunlight refracting into my eyes from a sea of high-rise buildings. It hurt; my eyes watered a little. An instant feeling of nostalgia washed over me, reflecting on a time that I was excited to be on the twenty-ninth floor of this stylish corporate building. A time I felt prestigious when I told people I worked here, when I shared the same eagerness for the company I'd grown to hate. Eileen was at my door; I took a deep breath, exhaling slowly, my shoulders dropping forward with the release of air.

'Where is the Balentine presentation?' she repeated as she turned the corner to my cubicle.

'They're right here. I'm just putting them in order, Eileen,' I said with a slightly higher pitched tone than usual. Hopefully she wouldn't suspect that I'd actually been asleep a few seconds ago. I slowly placed all the documents in a perfect pile on my desk as she waited, tapping her foot in anticipation.

'Coffee?' I asked, as I got up and handed her the papers, knowing I probably shouldn't have another one.

'Thanks, Kate, I'm in need of one,' she replied sternly as she grabbed the pile from my hand. She veered back toward her office as quickly as she came, as I headed in the opposite direction. I made my way to the kitchen, going through the foyer and passing the large round stainless-steel clock on the wall, its *tick-tock* echoing through our cubicles. The kitchen sink was full of dirty dishes again. I never understood why no-one ever cleaned up after themselves, always waiting for the receptionist to do it at the end of the day.

It was 2:35pm on an overcast fall Tuesday. I only had another three hours to go before I could escape from this place. Then it would be Wednesday, hump day, the halfway mark reminding me the weekend is just around the corner. It annoyed me that I had started thinking this way, counting down the days until the weekend and working in a field that I wasn't passionate about anymore. *When did I choose this life? When did I become so unhappy?* These questions came to me more frequently these days. I gave Eileen her coffee and went back to my desk, continuing to stare out of the window, watching the tiny ant-sized people scurry through the streets. It was only 2:47pm.

Da ding da ding da ding! My own alarm startled me. It was 4:55pm, and in around four minutes I could make my discreet getaway. I'd been doing this for some time now and nobody had said anything, or maybe nobody really cared. The receptionist was always loading the dishwasher, making it the perfect time to escape. At precisely 4:59pm I hurried down the elevator, power walked through the busy streets and hoped I wouldn't miss the earlier train even though I had to squeeze through every other person in the city who had the exact same idea as me. I jogged a little – well, I guess it was more of a canter – and when I finally got to the bottom of the stairs, I was glad to see I'd made my usual train. Sucking my stomach in and holding my breath, I managed to squeeze next to a construction worker and a well-dressed businessman, leaning closer toward the latter, presuming he smelt a little nicer. I was right. The train stopped, and just like every other day, a wave of relief rushed over me as I got closer to home, looking forward to the greeting I would receive when I opened the front door.

'Baaabbby!' I squealed, walking through the door and seeing my little French bulldog bounding toward me with a wagging tail and enough saliva to drown me. I kicked off my three-inch black heels, unclipped my bra, pulled my white blouse from my black pencil skirt that I unzipped and let fall to the floor, ready to embrace her.

'Where's Daddy?' I asked her, scratching the back of her ear and letting her lick my chin. Mark wasn't home yet. He hadn't been home early for months now. I tilted my head to the side and gave Luna a sad face, I'm sure she missed Mark being around just as much as I did. Mark worked a lot harder than me. I mean, I *worked*, but I was one of those people who, if I won the lotto, would go to work and tell everyone that bothered me exactly what I thought of them. I'd live the rest of my days on a big white yacht with people feeding me grapes while draped in the most expensive silk money could buy. Mark, on the other hand, would invest that money and probably stop working overtime. No. He would still work overtime, just less overtime … maybe. I picked up the phone and dialled his number with a canny grin, amused by my own thoughts.

'How's my beautiful lady doing?'

'I'm fine. How're you? Are you working late tonight?'

'Yes, I have to finish this case soon and only just noticed the time. How was your day?'

I still loved that Mark would ask unfailingly how I was and how my day went. It had been eight years, but this simple question made my heart smile every time.

'Oh, you know, the same as usual. I drank far too much coffee and can't get the ringing of Eileen's voice out of my ears,' I said sarcastically. 'So, will you be home for dinner tonight?' I heard Mark hesitate. He didn't need to say much more, I already knew what that meant.

'That's okay, I know you're busy with the case. I'll leave a plate in the oven for you.'

'Thanks. I better go. I'll finish this as quickly as I can and come home. Love you!'

'I love you too,' I said, hanging up the phone, sad that I couldn't have dinner with Mark. Again. It was more than him not being home for dinner, though; I hated being home alone more than anything else. I turned on the TV for some white noise and scrolled through social media while pouring myself a glass of red wine. Mark always preferred home-cooked meals, and most of the time I enjoyed doing that for him, but not tonight. Tonight, I felt like some comfort food, like some of my favourite pizza.

Ring, ring, ring, ring! I already knew who was going to pick up the phone.

'Hi, Sal. Can I order a medium margherita please? Half with pineapple.'

'Kate?' Salvatore asked.

'Yes, Salvatore, Mark is working late again.'

'Again? That man needs to spend time with his wife!'

'We aren't married, Sal, maybe you can throw in some garlic bread for saying such ridiculous things?' I joked, but I also knew he would.

'Sure, sure,' he said with a laugh in his thick Italian accent. 'I'll get Ginny to bring it up to you in about twenty minutes, okay?'

'Thanks, Sal!' I hung up the phone. Mark and I had been living in a modest-sized Manhattan apartment, and even though I never told Mark, it was definitely Salvatore's pizza joint connected to the lobby of the building that swayed my decision to move here. It reminded me of home – of Brooklyn. I looked over at Luna sitting quietly on the couch.

'It looks like it's just you and me again tonight, Loons!' I said, lying on the couch next to her. We exchanged disappointed looks and I turned back to my phone, scrolling through stories and posts of couples having dinner together, women being boss babes and Melanie from high school that I hadn't seen in ten years in her two-piece gym outfit drinking a protein shake *#fitbodgoals*. I threw my phone to the other side of the couch and hugged Luna a little closer. *I guess I should be used to this.*

2

Dreams

That night I had a vivid dream about Mark. I dreamt about the first time I met him. It was at an Irish pub in our early twenties for the end-of-exam party. I was with my best friend, Adeline, and he was with his younger brother, Chad. We didn't know each other, but I'd seen him around campus. He didn't dress like the other rich jocks; he had a cool, nonchalant appeal about him. The last time I passed him, I told myself one day I would meet him. I didn't know when, but I knew it would happen. I distinctly remember his smile as we locked eyes that night in the pub. I remember it like it was yesterday. Chad was talking to some preppy-looking girl, and Adeline had just seen a friend she wanted to quickly chat to, so it was the perfect opportunity to approach him. Being a few drinks deep at that point, I wasn't lacking any confidence. I held my brand-new camera and brazenly walked up to him to ask if I could take his picture. I told him I was taking photos for the school newspaper. Our school didn't have a newspaper, but he didn't need to know that. I loved his smile, and I wanted to capture it. We talked about his brother, Chad, who was in my year, but I made it clear that I was interested in him. I liked mature guys. Mark was mature.

He oozed dominance and masculinity, and unlike Chad, the beautiful girls doing tequila shots at the bar didn't faze him. I liked that. He was a thinker, an analyst, the kind of guy that knew where he was going. He would always be that person standing in the back corner, taking everything in and watching the events unfold, never to be made a fool of or lose his self-control.

I woke up for a second, wriggled myself into a comfier position and effortlessly fell back to sleep.

Then I dreamt about the day he asked me out. How I called Adeline straightaway and told her I had met 'the one'. I had. He used to stand close to me and whisper in my ear just because he knew it made my knees go weak. I remembered how everyone in the room would disappear when we kissed and how the world felt like it would stop moving when we were having sex. It was intense. In my eyes, he was perfection. He was my kind of perfect. The dream felt so real, like I was falling in love for the very first time again, but then it all started warping and I was having flashes of our life together, but this time it felt eerie, it didn't feel exhilarating and exciting anymore. I could see it all in front of me; all the road trips we had been on, our hiking adventures, the time we spent all night writing down places we would one day go together, but then suddenly, we were in Mexico, walking on the beach and fighting about leaving the resort, the camera hanging from my neck fell to the floor and shattered. I instantly felt empty.

I woke up abruptly, thinking it was because of the dark turn the dream took. I was about to reposition myself to get back to sleep when I started thinking about the camera.

Gosh. That camera. Mom bought me that brand-new camera for my birthday, she knew how much I loved photography and she always told me I had a good eye for it. I smiled thinking about it, rolling over instinctively to cuddle Mark, but he wasn't there. It was empty and the bedsheets were cold. My smile disappeared. *Did he not come home last night?* Sitting up, I rubbed my eyes with my hands and looked around, hoping he had.

The first thing I noticed was his work shirt – it was lying on the ground along with the pants he had stepped out of near the ensuite door, and I knew that hadn't been there when I went to bed. Then I heard the sound of the coffee machine. Mark was frothing the milk. I got out of bed and went downstairs. I saw the time on the microwave.

'Babe, it's 5:45am. Why are you going back to work so early?' I asked mid-yawn, stretching my arms above my head, my purple silk robe tied around my waist loosening a little.

'Sorry! I woke you up, didn't I?' he said, pulling an apologetic face, his bottom teeth showing as he stretched his bottom lip and chin in a downward motion.

'I don't think so. I was dreaming and woke up just before I heard the coffee machine.' I walked up to him and kissed behind his neck, moving my hands down his back and gesturing for a little more, but he shrugged me away.

'I need to get to work. Tonight though, okay?' he kissed me on the cheek. 'What did you dream about?' he asked, sipping his coffee in one hand and attempting to fix his tie with the other.

'It was about our trip to Mexico. We haven't been anywhere in such a long time, maybe we should plan something soon?' I said, looking up at him hopefully. But I already knew his response before he gave it to me.

'You know I'm not in a position to at the moment, not if I want to make partner.'

'I know; I hope you get it soon. You've been working so hard for it!' Not wanting to sound whiny, I decided to drop the subject. Instead, I started making myself a coffee. *Leave it. Don't bring it up. Don't do it.* I tried to supress my thoughts and feelings, but I couldn't.

'What if you get the promotion, though, won't you have more responsibility and possibly longer hours? Maybe we should go now before that happens.' I said in the most casual voice possible, completely dialling down how much I wanted this.

'I haven't even got it yet, and I can't take that chance, Kate. Imagine if I came back and Craig got the promotion. I've worked so hard for it!'

Well, I guess it was worth another try. He was right, I guess. Mark gulped down his coffee, threw on his suit jacket, grabbed his briefcase, kissed me on the cheek and was out the door. He didn't miss a step, like clockwork.

'I'll call you when I get into the office,' he added, before the door slammed shut behind him. The emptiness I felt when I first woke up set in again. I finished making my coffee and walked over to the couch where Luna was sleeping and lay next to her, petting her ear.

'Is this it?' I asked her, wishing she could respond.

She opened her eyes, just staring into mine for a moment, making a little sound, like she was telling me it was going to be alright. Then she curled up and went back to sleep. I continued to lie there next to her. *Is it really going to be okay?*

3

Questions

I found myself pondering life a lot that week, thinking about past decisions – good and bad. Those fork-in-the-road moments that apparently lead you to exactly where you're supposed to be. Sometimes I look back and wonder how certain decisions have led me to this point. *If I hadn't met Mark, where would I be now? What kind of person would I have become? Would I be leading the same life and doing the same menial job? The only difference being, I would leave the office and return to an empty home? Or be living and loving someone else?*

It had me thinking about my father, wondering if he had been a better one, maybe I would have been a different person altogether. A stronger, more confident and self-assured woman who follows her dreams and lives life to the absolute fullest. There were only a few memories I had of him, like that Christmas Eve when my parents were together. That was my last memory of them at their happiest. I must have been around six years old. He snuck into my room and put glow-in-the-dark stars on my ceiling and told me that Santa Claus had left them there for me. I used to have reoccurring nightmares and would wake up in a cold sweat. He taught me to count the stars whenever I felt afraid or had a bad dream. I knew Dad had stuck them there in the first place, but I didn't want to hurt his feelings. Every night I would go to sleep and the ceiling would illuminate with our solar system, it always made me wonder how tiny we must be, each person like a fleck of dust on earth.

Looking back, I must have been pretty darn bright to be contemplating human existence at that age. It was one of the few good memories I had of him, so I hung onto it. This is not to say I had the worst childhood in the world – I didn't. I knew it could have been worse. Both my parents loved me and migrated to the 'Land of the Great' to provide a better future for me and my two siblings. *I wonder if they knew how the stress of immigration and adapting to a completely different culture was going to impact them, and if they knew, would they have still done it?*

I remember Mom being sweet and caring when I was younger, but she changed radically after the divorce from the nurturing woman that had held me close. She developed a hard skin and had this incredible fighting resilience. I couldn't blame her for changing; I know there's no guidebook to dealing with immigration, parenting and divorce. There were times when I'd get home from school to find Mom buried in paperwork and crying over the finances. Of course, being so young and naive, I didn't know what any of this meant. To me, Mom and Dad were apart for a bit and doing their own thing for a while. But I often look back and wonder at what point did they realise it wasn't working. *When did they fall out of love?*

My relatives always spoke so positively of their relationship, almost like this surreal fairytale romance. She was smitten for him, and he, the fun party lover, felt the same for her. *Where did it all go wrong? How did she end up single-handedly having to raise three children in a new country on less than minimum wage? When did that love turn into violence and abuse?* I remember him hitting her in another room one day after school; she was screaming and crying for him to stop. He didn't. The sound of her being pushed against the wardrobe door still makes the hairs on my arms stand up – in fact, anyone raising their voice still makes my hair stand on end.

Mark never raises his voice. I remember a muffled sound coming from their bedroom, trying desperately to fall asleep so I didn't have to hear it anymore. I still hear the sound of Mom's voice through the tears and fear like it was yesterday. But I would just do as Dad told me and count the stars until I fell asleep. Sometimes, Dad would come into our bedroom late at night, waking us up, telling us to go and hug Mom better. *Were we the reason she was crying? Maybe we were the reason he was hurting her? It was our fault, and we must kiss Mommy better.*

It was one hot sunny day, during a typical New York heatwave, when she told him we were going swimming, and that was the day we ran away from him. She had five dollars in her pocket and three children she wanted to protect. To this day, the image of him sitting in the spare room asking me not to go swimming with her is so clear in my mind. *What would have happened if I stayed?* We spent weekends with him until we legally didn't have to. It was more fun hanging out with friends after that. At eighteen, I took the opportunity to not go back, glad to never be told I was the 'woman of the house' that needed to cook frozen pies and pizzas for him and my siblings again.

The miniscule relationship we had shrunk into non-existence, and the most unfortunate part of that is how it probably affected me without anyone even realising. It took me a long time to trust Mark, and he would always tell me it was my dad's fault for not caring for me properly, not stepping up to his responsibilities. I didn't know how a relationship with a man worked, how it was supposed to feel. Mark did more than just help me reflect and move on from my trauma, he looked after me, he shaped me, he moulded me. I stepped away from my self-abusive nature and surrendered to becoming the perfect partner for him. I knew we wouldn't end up like my parents, and that's all that really mattered.

Quite frankly, I always wondered how a messed-up girl from a broken home could find and keep such a smart, successful man like him. I didn't realise it at the time, but Mark also came into my life at a pivotal moment. I had finished my final exams for the year and nearly dropped out of business school to study photography at college instead. I figured I could work part-time in an art gallery for extra cash because having a career in finance didn't really interest me. Mom liked the idea; she had always supported my photography and that I should focus my time on something I enjoyed.

'Yeah, but look where your mom is. Do you want to end up like her, she's always broke?' he would say. I didn't. 'You are one of the few fortunate people that are good at numbers, the money will be way more secure than taking photos for fun. Do it as a hobby?' he said one night.

He was right, though, wasn't he? I didn't want to end up like Mom, only just managing to pay my bills and living pay cheque to pay cheque.

I never told Mom what he said, but she respected my decision to study business and finance. From that decision on, Mark was my biggest influence, and I would trust his opinions and choices more than my own. I was a different person, not for better or for worse, just different. I was no longer the party girl who could open beer bottles with her teeth. I was no longer the life and soul of the party. I was excited to be the wife of a future lawyer. We would have a beautiful home with financial security, two children and a dog. It would be perfect.

'Baby got back,' the tune started ringing.

My thoughts derailed as I heard the familiar sound of the Sir Mix-a-Lot song as someone's ringtone. I snapped back to reality and looked around, realising I had nearly missed my stop. I ran through the closing subway doors and quickly re-centred myself. *That was close.* I started walking through the sea of black business suits and looked around, feeling hot and bothered on the crisp morning. I was the partner of a well-respected lawyer; we did have beautiful, nice cars. We had Luna too. *So, why don't I feel happy?* And as if my question had been answered, I received a phone call.

'Kate?'

'Hi, Mom, I was just thinking about you!'

'Well, that can't be a good thing; what's wrong?'

'Why would you think something is wrong?'

'Oh, I don't know, maybe because I carried you in my womb for nine months,' she said for the millionth time, a joke so old I chuckled out of necessity.

'Are you coming into the city anytime soon, we should have lunch?'

'I actually called you because I'm coming into the city today and wanted to know where you bought that tea you drink from?'

'Oh, it's near my work, I'll pick you up a box. See you at lunch then?'

'Yes, see you then, chookie!' she said before I hung up the phone and continued my walk to work. *Maybe Mom will give me some good advice?*

4

Mom

The morning went by slowly, and I found myself continuously looking at the time. The more I looked, the slower it seemed to go. At 11:45am I had had enough, so I decided to go and buy the tea Mom wanted. As soon as I walked out of the office, she called, and I already knew why.

'Hi, Mom, what is the closest shop to you? I'm on my way!'

'Umm, I guess I'm next to that coffee place we went that one time?' she responded, her voice sounding slightly flustered. Mom didn't come into the city very much; she re-married a countryman and they retreated to upstate New York. It was quiet there, just the way they liked it, but she got overwhelmed each time she came back.

'Don't move. I'll be there in about five.'

'Okay, see you soon!' I already knew she wasn't going to stay still like I had asked; she wasn't the most patient person and was usually a liability in busy places, between knocking things over and always getting lost.

'Mom, I told you to wait at the coffee shop.'

'I knew you would have found me eventually,' she responded, inhaling the scent of the last pumpkin spice candle sitting in a small boutique store. We were three shops down from the coffee shop she said she would wait in, and I had to search each one to find her.

'I have to be back in fifty minutes you know?'

'Oh, alright then!' she put the candle back next to all the other festive scented candles and headed back to the cafe on Lexington Avenue.

'So, are you going to tell me what's on your mind?' she asked inquisitively, tilting her head to the left and raising both eyebrows. I avoided giving her an answer and instead passed her the menu.

'I'm going to get the turkey salad,' I said, gesturing for her to hurry. The waitress introduced herself, and after placing my order, we both stared at Mom eagerly.

'I'll just get a cream cheese bagel, thanks,' she said, folding the menu back up. The waitress nodded and walked away.

'Mom, do you think Mark and I are meant to be together?' I asked, the depths of me knowing what a heavily loaded question it was. She was the one that didn't respond quickly this time.

'Where is this coming from?' she asked.

'I've been feeling a bit low. Mark is never home so we never do anything together or go away. I hate my job. I feel like we strived for so long and we have everything we wanted, but I still feel so empty!' I blurted out, my head now in my hands. I could have burst into tears then and there, but I kept it in. Mom had that concerned look on her face, which made me feel even more anxious.

'I don't know what you want me to say,' she responded.

'Do you think he is the one for me?'

'I don't think I can answer that for you, Katie,' she said as she started bending the corners of her menu. 'Mark is a lovely man, he would do anything for you, and I know he loves you madly …' she trailed off, not finishing her sentence.

'Is that all I need?' I asked her, wanting more, 'Is that really enough?'

'I can't answer that for you. I think you should talk to Mark about how you are feeling.'

'I guess … I just don't know how to talk to him about this sort of thing. He's so occupied with this promotion at the moment,' I said sadly. There was a long awkward silence, which was broken when the waitress offered a steaming cup of their fresh house coffee. We asked for a Seltzer instead.

'Sorry, I didn't mean to push this on you today,' I said sheepishly, forcing a smile on my face to break the tension.

'Oh, love, you can talk to me about anything. You know, I stuck around with your father for years even though he was totally wrong for me. I was so scared to leave him because of what people might think, and I had no idea what I was going to do with myself, especially with three children. It was thanks to your Uncle Patrick, who was always travelling around the world and sending your father letters and photos that made me realise how much life there was out there in the world.' I looked up at her, as she stared deeply yet calmly into my eyes. 'Your uncle knew what I was going through, and when your father was at work, he would often call me to ask how I was doing, telling me that he would support me if I chose to leave.' Mom had never spoken about this before, so I was curious as to why she was bringing it up now. Her eyes were glistening. *Is she about to cry?*

'Is that why you left Dad, because of my uncle?'

'The last time your father hit me was because he suspected something was going on between us. He hit me so hard I fell to the floor, and I could barely move my jaw the next day. There was something different about that last time. We left him the next day.'

'Is that the day you took us swimming?' I asked.

'You remember that?' she asked, looking confused.

'I don't remember much. I just remember Dad asking me to stay behind with him, but you told me to hurry up and get in the car or we would be late for lessons.'

'Do you remember where we went?' she asked, but I shook my head. 'We stayed with Patrick for a little while, and your father never spoke to him again.'

'Were you and Patrick …?' I didn't finish my sentence, but Mom knew what I was asking.

'Oh no, not at all,' she said while fidgeting with the button on her jacket pocket. 'But I was very fond of Patrick; he's a good man, sometimes I wonder if I picked the wrong brother.'

'I don't remember living with him.' I was trying desperately hard to remember his house, our refuge, but nothing came to me.

'His place was interesting. He had all these photos pinned on the wall of people he'd met, and little trinkets he used to collect on his trips.'

'Where is he now?'

'He moved to Scotland when I was back on my feet, but I haven't heard from him since. I suppose he's in touch with your father now, but I wouldn't know.' She started playing with a charm on her bracelet. I'd never noticed it before. I took her hand and admired the sparkling silver bead on her wrist, next to the others she had collected over the years.

'It's a Scottish thistle. He gave it to me before he left and told me to visit.'

'Did you ever visit?' I asked her, hoping she would say she had, but with sadness in her eyes, she shook her head.

'How have I never known this before?' I asked her, surprised and a little hurt she hadn't told me sooner.

'Well, you never asked,' she said, shrugging and sitting up in her chair, clearly wanting to change the subject.

'Have you ever tried to get in contact with him?'

'This was a lifetime ago now,' she paused, 'and what would I have said anyway?' *Maybe, thank you? Maybe, how are you?* Mom was clearly upset, and I didn't want to press the issue; instead, I left the lightly planted seed for another day. As the waitress placed our meals in front of us, I realised why Mom had shared this story after nearly thirty years. Regret. Fear.

'Mom,' I said, taking her hands and smiling at her, 'it's never too late, you know?' She took a deep breath in and shrugged the tension out of her as she exhaled.

'I guess the best advice I can give you is don't make decisions based on fear like I did.' I passed her the salt and pepper from the holder next to us and gestured to eat, knowing I didn't have long of my lunchbreak left. We ate in silence and walked back to my office slowly, arm in arm.

'After everything with Dad, was it hard to let Derrick into your life?'

Mom laughed, purely at the thought of Derrick, I'm sure. It was a cheeky and hearty laugh. 'Not really, it felt right. Even if I had to go through it all again, just to end up with a man like him, I would in a heartbeat.' We were finally at the front of my office and the last place I wanted to be.

'I really wish we could do this more often,' I said to her, taking her into my arms and hugging her warmly.

'I know, why you don't come up for the weekend, we can have a nice girly time, invite your sister?'

'Yeah, I'll let you know, I promise. Thanks, Mom.'

I walked through the big revolving doors and to the elevators, thinking about what Mom's life would have been like if she went to Scotland. *Would she have only visited? Would we have moved there?* I sat back at my desk, wondering what it would have felt like to grow up with uncles, aunties and cousins ...

5

Signs

The talk with Mom hadn't made my decision any easier; it evoked wanting change, that feeling that I was ready for something more, something exciting. It made me feel that maybe Mark wasn't the issue. *Maybe I just need more adventure? Maybe I need to make a change in my own life unrelated to him?* It hadn't occurred to me before, but somehow, getting a fancy car, a mortgage and a nine-to-five stable job became more important than doing the things that brought me joy like travel and photography. I stared into the sea of grey buildings ahead of me, like cemetery headstones clustered together, one after another, the grey clouds blending into the buildings with no colour in sight. I was doing that a lot those days, easily lost in my own downward spiral of thoughts and falling into some kind of daze, struggling to be present.

Swivelling my chair back to the computer, I started searching random destinations to travel to. *Scotland or Australia? Thailand? Or Africa?* I couldn't help but instantly smile as I looked at the magnificent landscapes, animals and tours each country had to offer.

It was the loud, fast footsteps coming toward my office that naturally shifted my thoughts back to reality. The swift pace and the distinct tap of how her heel hit the floor meant it was Eileen. I heavily exhaled, my chest dropping, and quickly minimised all the travel tabs on my computer, in case she decided to stand behind me. I grabbed the closest pen and started making random notes on a file that was in front of me.

1. tax department

2. motor vehicle

I had no idea what I was writing and realised a little too late that I probably should have opened the file itself.

'Okay, what's going on?' Eileen demanded with a firm voice, walking straight to the right side of my desk. I looked up to her as the scent of Chanel N°5 wafted in the air, her red lipstick bleeding slightly onto her skin with the corners of her mouth turned down.

'Sorry?' I asked, confused, as she placed a stack of papers on my desk with both hands, the weight of her body on them leaning forward, keeping them on the stack as she spoke. She didn't look impressed. I kept my eyes on the corner of her lip, watching it curve down further with every second.

'These Balentine financial statements went out completely wrong and the client sent it back with all the mistakes in red pen. Do you know how bad that looks for us?' She paused for a moment, but I knew that wasn't the end of it. 'Look, I know your mind has been somewhere else recently, but you have to focus. We can't afford to have any more mistakes like this, Katelyn. We can't have this kind of unbillable time.' She threw her hands in the air then, nearly knocking over the framed picture of Mark and Luna. 'I need all of this corrected and the amended copies on my desk before you go home today.'

Hurricane Eileen left just as quickly as it came, her scent lingering in the air. I sat for a moment, staring at the stack of white papers, flicking through the black, size ten Calibri words marked by red on every page. *Urgh. Maybe the contrasting colours make it look worse than it is?* I opened all the travel pages, hovered my cursor over the black 'x' and clicked. One by one, gone. *Goodbye, Scotland. Goodbye, Australia.* I didn't need any distractions. The last thing I wanted was to be unemployed. I opened the Balentine documents and began revising. That was the rest of my day. No coffee. No talking. No 4:55pm alarm to sneak out while the receptionist was loading the dishwasher. Amendment after amendment, only looking up when I heard the cleaners enter the floor and start vacuuming. It was 6:45pm when I finally finished, dropping the printed files to Eileen's office on my way out, embarrassed with the amount of corrections I needed to make and the time it took me.

'I'm all done. I'm really sorry about that, Eileen,' I said, looking down as she stopped what she was doing and looked sternly at me. It felt like I was in trouble at the principal's office.

'What's going on with you?' she asked. I was unsure if she was genuinely concerned. I kept my eyes on the tacky carpet, not knowing how to answer her and unable to make eye contact.

'I don't know,' I said under my breath, shrugging.

'Well, you need to figure it out. It's a busy time at the moment, and we don't have the resources to check your work!' I could tell she was tired and had enough of the day too, but my chest tightened a little, triggered by her words. *Does she even want to be here?* I took a deep breath in, and then out, hoping my breath would loosen my chest slightly.

'I know. I'll be more careful.' I turned to leave, but then turned back to her.

'Eileen, how much leave do I have? Maybe I should take some time off, come back refreshed?' I didn't even know where that question came from, and I definitely wasn't sure how she'd respond to it after what had happened today.

'I don't know. I would have to check,' she said, this time not looking up at me. The hair on the back of my neck stood up, and I started getting tingly with frustration.

Deep breaths, Katelyn, Eileen has had a tough day too. She knew I was still standing there and was probably waiting for me to leave. I didn't move.

'Maybe I could take a month off?' I probed, hoping for a reaction, or at least eye contact. Eileen lifted her head slowly, giving me the eye contact I decided I didn't want anymore. She took her glasses off and closed her eyes, pinching her nasal passage and scrunching her eyebrows together.

'Just like everybody else in the company, you've signed a contract that allows you a maximum of two weeks leave for the year. If you haven't taken it in the last year, that's all you have. There will be no exceptions for anybody.' Her eyes pierced mine. She put her glasses back on and returned to whatever she was doing.

'What if I wanted to take leave without pay? Would that be a possibility?' I continued. I knew I was pushing it, but what was the harm in asking, seeing as though we were on the topic anyway, then I wouldn't have to have this awkward conversation with her again. She took a moment before replying. *What is she thinking?*

'You would have to reapply for your job when you return.'

'Excuse me?' I was taken aback. 'I've been with this company for six years and I couldn't possibly take leave without pay for a slightly extended time?' I tried my best to keep my voice calm even though my heart had started beating a little faster. I could tell Eileen wanted this conversation to end just as much as I did. She shifted in her chair and ran her long red nails through her peroxide-white hair.

'It's in your contract, Katelyn. There are plenty of people out there that would give an arm and a leg for your position. If we bend the rules for you, everyone will want the rules bent for them. There will be no exceptions. I'm sorry.' It was not the response I was expecting. I could feel my face heat and tears start welling in my eyes. I held them back. I turned to leave, understanding her stance but also not wanting to cry there and then.

'In another year you'll be eligible for three weeks leave, maybe you should wait until then for a bigger trip?' she added, knowing the conversation was finally over, and possibly feeling empathetic to the situation. *Does she really think that is going to make me feel better?*

'Good to know. I'll see you tomorrow,' I said as I turned to walk out.

'Goodnight, Katelyn,' I heard her say softly.

As soon as I got outside, I burrowed my face in my hands, the cold air on my skin and the warm tears starting to fall like giant pellets of rain down my cheek, hitting my blouse. I walked slowly to the subway that night, not feeling any desire to rush. *Will it be another dinner alone anyway?* I looked up at the sky to try and stop my nose running, an instant sense of calm taking over my body. The stars reminded me of the glow-in-the-dark solar system on the ceiling of my childhood bedroom. I wished for something more, something different. *I can't do this anymore!* I was so busy screaming on the inside as I walked, I didn't hear what was happening on the outside.

'Excuse me, miss?' I heard someone say. I kept walking with my head down, assuming it hadn't been directed at me. 'Umm, excuse me?' The voice grew louder and was suddenly more direct. I looked up, annoyed someone had interrupted my depressive implosion. A young woman was standing in front of me. She had thick, curly black hair and a single freckle on her right cheek, her tanned skin glistening in the streetlights. She had a worn backpack strapped around her chest and waist suggesting she was a backpacker.

'Err, yes?' I responded calmly, looking at her confused. It was rare for a stranger to approach me, probably because I never responded to anyone while rushing through the city.

'Do you know where the night market is? I can't seem to find it, and I've been walking around for some time now,' she replied, rolling her eyes with a hint of embarrassment in her voice. She sounded Australian, or maybe South African, I couldn't tell.

'Oh, sure. Just follow this road for about three blocks and then turn right. You'll see plenty of lights at the end of the street when you turn.' I was pointing in the direction I wanted her to go in.

'Thanks so much, I appreciate it!' I watched her walk on, admiring her courage as what I assumed was a lone wolf, travelling alone.

'Hey!' I yelled as I quickly hurried after her, 'I may as well walk you to the corner, I have time to kill.' She didn't agree or disagree with me; she just smiled and kept on walking.

'What's your name?' she asked.

'Katelyn, what's yours?'

'Felicity.'

'It's nice to meet you. Whereabouts are you from?'

'Australia, I'm visiting a friend for a week,' she replied, rubbing her hands together to warm then.

'Australia! Amazing! I would love to go one day!' I told her.

'One day, huh? Everyone always says one day!' she said with a smile, jumping slightly to readjust her backpack. She was right. I've said one day for nearly ten years!

'Where in Australia?' I asked, assuming she would say Sydney or Melbourne.

'Perth.'

'Oh, I don't know where that is.' She didn't look offended. I wondered if she got that a lot. 'Can you see the lanterns a few blocks away?' I asked her, pointing ahead.

'Yes, I see them. I'll head there. Thanks so much for the company!' Felicity turned and unexpectedly hugged me. *Does she hug strangers often?* 'If you're ever in Perth, look me up! It's Felicity Williams.' She walked backwards for a few strides, waving goodbye to me, a little bounce to her step I wondered if I ever had. It had been a little while since I had walked this side of town, and a new shop grabbed my attention. I crossed the road and headed towards it. *Maybe it wasn't all that bad staying back late today?*

6

Jenny

Beeeeep. I stepped into the warm office, listening to the long chime that warned the blue-suited, happy-faced travel agents that a potential customer has walked in. I was a little nervous. I hadn't been into a travel agency since Mark and I booked our trip to Mexico. That was another lifetime – three years ago, to be exact. *Gosh. It's been that long? I haven't been anywhere for three years!* I wondered what Mark would think if he knew I was there, but I figured it was harmless. After all, I was just looking around to see if there were any deals, nothing serious, no commitments ...

I felt drawn to the pamphlets in the corner and picked one up that read *Tour of the Greek Islands* in big blue block letters, my eyes wandering to the deals on cruises that were blue-tacked to the wall.

'Hi, how are you?' someone said. I turned quickly, startled. A plump lady popped her head out of the door behind the desk, not too far from where I was standing. She was holding a cup of tea in one hand, with peach-coloured lipstick softly pressed around the rim where she'd been sipping, an indication she had been picking it up at different angles each sip. I don't think she expected anyone to come in so late.

'Are you closing? I can come back another time?' I asked politely, suddenly imagining Luna home alone again.

'Not at all. Please, take a seat,' she said, sitting at a chair behind the desk, ushering me to sit in front of her. 'How are you, love?'

'Good, and you?' I responded instinctively, not sure how I felt, a hint of apprehension in my voice. I felt resistance, potentially guilt, rushing over me, feeling I should be there with Mark.

'I'm ready for the weekend, to be quite honest with you!' I liked her candour, 'My name is Jenny. How can I help you today?' I watched her take another sip of tea.

'Umm, I'm not sure … I would like to go on a holiday, but if I'm honest, I don't really know where to start, it's been three years since I've travelled overseas and don't feel comfortable doing it myself online.' Jenny nodded politely, not saying anything as she started using the keyboard.

'No problem at all! Let's start with some simple questions. How long do you have?'

'About two weeks, up to about four max, I think, maybe,' I responded tensely, unsure.

'Perfect! Do you have anywhere in mind? What do you like doing?' She gently probed a little more, this time revealing some lipstick on her tooth as she spoke. She didn't feel pushy, but her bright blue eyes focusing on mine made me nervous. I didn't know the answer to these questions.

'Scotland. I have family there I would love to meet.' I found myself alarmed at what I naturally felt called to say.

'Okay, anywhere else?' she continued curiously. For some reason, the glow-in-the-dark stickers my father put up that Christmas came to my mind.

'I would love to see the northern lights?' I somewhat asked her, as she took another sip of her tea. Her eyes sparkled for a little moment as she continued typing.

'Well, how about Iceland and then Scotland?'

'What's in Iceland?' I asked her, never having really thought of it as a destination to visit. Rather than telling me, she showed me. She swivelled the screen of her computer toward me to reveal a woman in an outdoor turquoise pool, steam coming from the water like I had seen in Mexico. Above the woman on the screen, the sky lit up with green lights.

'Wow!' I smiled, still not really knowing anything about the place. Another picture in the corner of the screen caught my eye; it was two girls making a peace sign at the top of a mountain. Jenny followed my gaze.

'Oh, that's Diamond Head in Hawaii.'

'I want to go there too!' I said, smiling, just imagining what it would be like to stand at the top of a mountain. 'What beautiful mountain views!'

'Oh, that's not a mountain, that's the crater of a volcano.' *A volcano?* She must have noticed I looked embarrassed. 'It's okay. I didn't realise that until I was there myself!'

'You must have been to so many places?' I asked.

'I have, but there are still so many on my bucket list.'

It started bothering me that I had only been to an all-inclusive in Mexico with Mark in the last eight years.

'Where would you recommend going if you had to choose?'

She smiled and pointed back at the woman standing in the outdoor pool.

'That's where you have the best chance of seeing the northern lights – the aurora borealis.' She scrolled to another picture of it. A couple holding hands with fur-hooded jackets were embracing each other beneath the lights. I had goosebumps instantly. 'You don't even have to spend the whole time there, it's usually just a stopover for many, so would work well if you decide to head to the UK.' I didn't say anything; I was trying to keep my emotions under control instead of getting excited about something that may not materialise.

'I have family in Scotland, but I've never met them before.'

'Well, maybe this is the perfect time?'

It felt good to be there, sitting and talking to Jenny about the places I could go. It felt easy. It felt right. If I didn't feel the need to talk to Mark about it, I probably would have booked my trip there and then. I wasn't even sure he knew I had family there, it had only ever been my immediate family since we had been together. It's something we never really spoke about it, nor something he asked about. *Would he even want to meet them?* Jenny could tell I was getting a little overwhelmed.

'What's your name, by the way?' she asked purposefully, as if to break my train of thought.

'Oh, sorry! It's Katelyn,' I responded, refocusing.

'Lovely. Well, I think we've done plenty of brainstorming for today, Katelyn. Why don't you have a think about it? Get in touch with your family and I'll be in contact with you in a couple days with a few ideas and quotes?'

'That sounds like a good idea, how much do you think that will be?' I wanted to be prepared for Mark's questions when I told him about it tonight.

'I couldn't tell you right now, there are too many things we don't know yet. The type of accommodation, the kind of flight, if it's peak time.'

'I'm not sure if my partner will be coming, so just something simple that I could give to him would be really helpful,'

'I'll email you a quote based on a five-day stay in Iceland and a ten-day stay in Scotland and different options if you wanted to be able to change your flights around,'

'Thank you, I really do appreciate it!' I wrote down my details for her as she gathered brochures on Iceland, Scotland and Hawaii.

'Take some of these and read through them. Send me an email about anything else you might be interested in, and we will go from there!' She handed me all the brochures she selected along with her business card, and I put them in my purse. 'Email me if you have any questions, okay?'

'Thanks so much!' I said, walking toward the door, becoming eager and excited to get home and tell Mark.

'Oh, and, Katelyn?' I turned around and looked back at Jenny. She was dangling the now-empty mug with her fingers and standing up from the seat. 'I'm sure your family would love to meet you!' We exchanged smiles as I stepped outside, hearing the subtle chime ring in the distance as I walked away.

I had butterflies. I couldn't remember the last time I had butterflies, but I liked it. I made my way towards the nearest subway. *Maybe today Mark got the promotion and work might be open to him taking a sabbatical? Maybe we could finally jet off on a holiday together? Maybe I just needed to take action?*

7

Decisions

Who knows what time it was when I finally got home, but I was surprised to see Mark's shoes by the doorway when I walked in. A part of me was glad he was home so that I could tell him about Jenny right then and there, not over the phone or the next time I saw him. Another part of me was worried and wished he were still at work so I didn't have to bring it up. I kept my mind focused on all the potential places we could go together and remembered I was speaking to the same man who once talked with me for hours about all the places we were going to visit. My heart started beating faster with the thought of being able to experience what was once a dream – or at least put something into motion, if nothing else. We would figure something out, even if he did give me the 'I'm-making-partner' speech again. As I continued walking through the apartment, my energy disappeared and was replaced with doubt.

The room was unusually dark and quiet for the fact that Mark was home; the air felt tense. Luna hadn't run up to me yet either. *Where are they?* I slowly closed my purse, hiding the brochures, and placed my purse on the couch as I walked towards the kitchen.

'Mark?' I called out, walking very cautiously. Luna made a sound. Only the kitchen spotlights were on, but I could see Mark sitting slumped at the dining table, a wine glass in one hand and an open bottle of wine on the table. Luna made another noise and then lay her head back on her paws by Mark's feet, offering her unconditional love and support to him, the way she always did. Mark didn't look up. He didn't need to.

'Mark? What's wrong? What happened? Is everything okay?' I rushed toward him, dragging the closest chair next to him. I put my hand on his leg, squeezing it gently so he knew I was there.

'Craig got the promotion,' he finally said as he looked up at me, his eyes full of disappointment and bitterness. He was devastated. I was devastated for him.

'What? You've worked so hard! Did they say why?' I spoke quickly but softly, trying to not sound whiny, not wanting to add any more frustration to the matter.

'No, they just said that's what the majority voted.' I knew there weren't any words I could say to make him feel better, so I stood up and started rubbing his shoulders and neck. We remained in silence.

'Let's go out for dinner?' I suggested, trying to change his mood the only way I knew how.

'Why? There's nothing to celebrate,' he said, almost annoyed I suggested it.

'We are alive, we are well … Let's go out tonight; let's get out of the house. I don't feel like cooking and it's rare you are ever at home this early,' I said.

I walked to the closet and removed his coat from the hanger and put it on the dining table. Mark didn't move or say a word. I sighed, pulling him off the chair to stand and wrapped his arms around my neck, kissing him first on the lips, then on the nose and then on the forehead.

'Mark, talk to your boss, and if there isn't anything they can do then maybe it's time to look elsewhere. You are one of the few people I know that genuinely loves their job. You care so much about your clients, so keep doing what you're doing and something good will come from it.

There is a better opportunity waiting for you. There is a reason you didn't get this,' I said to him with a soft yet motivating voice.

'I guess,' he said, before returning my kiss. I could tell he didn't want to talk about it anymore. He took a deep breath. 'Okay!' he continued, 'Let's stay in, though. I feel like being at home right now. We'll throw something together quickly.'

He handed me his wine glass and walked over to the fridge. I already knew what 'we' planned to make for dinner, because it was the only thing he knew how to make. 'Mexican?' he yelled out as he took out two pieces of chicken breast, a pepper and tortillas from the fridge.

'Hmmm, fajitas?' I chuckled, taking a sip of his wine and putting his coat away again. This was the only reason we kept fajita mix in the pantry cupboard – for days like this.

I put some music on and walked over to Mark who had started slicing the chicken. 'This is nice, I can't remember the last time we did this,' I said, starting to slice the pepper next to him and wondering if I should tell him about meeting Jenny.

'Lucky for me, Craig can't get promoted any higher,' he said, meaning for it to sound playful.

'Let's just enjoy this for a moment; no Craig talk, okay?'

'Fine ... so, what's been up with you?' he asked.

'What do you mean?' Unsure what he meant, carefully trying to put my thoughts into words so it wouldn't spark any more emotional roller-coasters for the night.

'I know I've barely been around, but I've noticed you've been somewhere else lately,' he said, still cutting the chicken. I didn't respond so he took that as a cue to continue. 'I'm sorry for only focusing on becoming partner, I know I haven't given you much of my time ...' I didn't know if it was an appropriate time to tell him the truth or if it was a better idea to tell a little white lie after everything that had happened today.

'I know, honey, I understand,' I said quietly in response.

'Is there anything you want to talk about?' he prodded. I was screaming everything I wanted to say in my head, but nothing came out. He stopped cutting the chicken and this time he turned toward me, putting his hands on my shoulders and pulling me toward him so I was facing him. 'Talk to me, what's going on?' he looked at me with those beautiful dark brown eyes, wide with curiosity. I couldn't lie to him. And just like that, everything came out.

'I can't stop thinking about how we had such big dreams to see the world and we haven't done any of it,' I burst out, dropping my head down like I had said something wrong.

'We went to Mexico?' he said, clearly looking like he had solved all of our problems. I stared at him, dumbfounded.

'To Mexico … once … for our five-year anniversary … three years ago! And it was an all-inclusive holiday. What did we even experience?' My pitch got higher, clearly unimpressed by his response. 'It has honestly been consuming me, I need to get out of here, I need to go away and tick something off my bucket list! I feel like my life is wasting away!' His carelessness made me feel dramatic, but I knew I was ready for a change, for some adventure. *Am I wrong to feel this way?*

'Maybe you should go, then?' Mark responded calmy, catching me off guard. I didn't know if he was joking or being passive aggressive. It sounded real.

'What? You will take time off work?' I asked him, trying to decipher his words. Mark shook his head.

'No, maybe *you* should go.' He accentuated the *you* this time.

'By myself? Why won't you come with me?'

'Right now, I really need to focus on becoming partner, Katie. When I make partner, I promise I will spend time travelling with you.' He said it so confidently that I almost believed him again. I could feel tingling on the back of my neck, the same tingling I felt when Eileen and I had spoken before I left the office. I was upset he had already said no without any hesitation. I didn't respond. He knew me too well; he knew I was getting upset.

'It's just not something I'm thinking about right now, Kate, but you are, so maybe you should get it out of your system and then we can go back to normal? Maybe this is something you need to do for you?' It's hard to get angry when someone is telling you what you kind of want to hear. I got my cake, but I wanted to eat it too. And … *normal?* I wanted to ask him what 'normal' even meant but I didn't know if that would help or aggravate the situation. I decided to keep it to the discussion at hand, knowing full well I would go down a rabbit hole of 'normal' later.

'You really think so? You think that's a good idea?' I asked him, partly hoping he was joking and would turn around and say 'yes, of course I will come'. He didn't.

'I think if you want to do it, you should do it.'

I sighed, unsure if it was due to disappointment he didn't want to come or relief that he was at least fine with me going. It was enough of a prod for me to take his advice, though. *Mark might be able to wait for some ambiguous date in the future, but I'm not going to.* He put his arms around me and hugged me as I nestled my head into the crevice of his neck. We embraced for a few moments, feeling the warmth of his body radiate into mine.

'Okay. I'm starving now!' I exclaimed, kissing him on the lips as a call to action, back to cooking dinner, back to overanalysing 'normal'. *Is this our normal? Do I want this normal?*

8

Strife

It was unusual waking up to Mark still in bed on a Saturday morning. Usually, his alarm would wake me, and I would remain in bed chatting to him while he got ready for a 'few things he needed to finish up at the office'. That really meant he would be there all day. It was nice to wake up naturally with the intimacy of feeling someone next to me in bed.

'Good morning,' he said, pulling me closer to him.

'I can't remember the last time I woke up to this,' revealing my thoughts to him, turning around and pressing my body on his, kissing him on the lips. 'I could get used to this,' I whispered. It was devastating to think that losing the promotion allowed us time to connect again. 'Are you going in today?' I asked him, before I got too excited that I could hold on to his body and the feeling a little longer.

'No, not today. I don't want to see Craig right now. I don't want to see any of them right now.' I could tell Mark was imagining their faces.

'What do you want to do today, then?' I asked.

'I'm not sure, what should we do?'

I gave him a cheeky look and crawled on top of him, my legs spread over his waist, kissing his neck and lightly biting his earlobe. He chuckled nervously and gently moved me off him.

'Come on, Mark, it's been so long.' I tried again, moving my hands beneath the sheets. I felt him give in for a moment, his exhale relaxing his neck and chest. I kissed down his neck and went to straddle him once more hoping he would surrender fully.

'Katie,' he started saying, wriggling away.

'What's wrong?' I was confused and embarrassed.

'Nothing, I'm just a bit upset with everything that happened at work, I can't concentrate on this right now.'

'I don't want you to concentrate right now, I want you to relax. I want you to finally relax.' I held his face in the palms of my hands and kissed him on the lips, but this time he didn't return it.

'I need some space right now.' He rubbed his face, and without saying another word, ripped back the sheets and walked to the ensuite, closing the door behind him. *What just happened?*

I didn't know what to do, sitting in bed and staring at the closed ensuite door. *Did I do something wrong? Did I come on too strong? Do I not turn him on anymore?* Even with all the questions swarming through my mind, I decided not to push him. *Maybe he is very stressed? Maybe the time apart has made him nervous to perform?*

I got out of bed and stood by the closed door, leaning my head against it.

'Mark?' I said softly. 'I'm sorry if it felt a bit pushy, I didn't mean to upset you. Let's leave it. How about we go out for breakfast? Let's take Luna too?'

After what felt like an eternity, he opened the door and sheepishly stood there nodding.

I watched him as he walked toward the closet, hoping he would get back into bed, or show some kind of affection toward me, maybe even an apology. He didn't. He was getting ready, so I followed suit, trying not to think about what had happened. I took extra time staring at myself in the mirror, trying to make sense of it all. I eyed myself up and down, disappointed at how messy my hair looked, how the bottom of my belly poked out and the cellulite on my butt. It was true, I guess. I didn't do my hair anymore. I never bought new lingerie or clothes. *Maybe that's what I need to do for Mark? I'll shave my legs and dress sexy. Surely that'll do it?*

9

Girls

Breakfast didn't go as I imagined; we sat in silence for the most part, and I was grateful when I got a call from my best friend, Adeline.

'Kate! Where have you been?' she said as soon as I picked up.

'No "hello"?' I chuckled, 'Sorry, girl, work has been ridiculously busy. What's up with you?'

'Checking in to see if you were going to Eva's bachelorette party next weekend?'

'Oh gosh, I totally forgot about that! It's next weekend? Where is it again? It was out of town, right?'

'It's next Friday and Saturday night in Niagara. I think she has a wine tour booked and then something in the evening?'

'Ahhh, I will ask Mark and see what he says.'

'Really? Permission?' she annoyingly sung to me. I could hear her groan as I got off the phone, but I hadn't told her what had happened with Mark and the promotion, so I didn't expect her to understand why I felt the need to.

'Adeline?' Mark asked me as I got off the phone.

'Yeah, she called to ask if I was going to Eva's bachelorette party next weekend.'

'Oh, yeah, I don't know if I'll go to the bachelor party. I don't really speak to those guys!'

'Maybe you should? Get out, have some fun. I think it's here in the city.'

'Maybe, I'll look at the invite. What're you guys up to?'

'We're going to Niagara next Friday. I'll have to take a half-day off work, stay Friday and Saturday night then come back on the Sunday. Did you want me to not go? We could go away instead and have some quality time?' I said, looking at him playfully.

'You can't miss your friend's bachelorette party!' He was right, I couldn't remember the last time we had a girls' trip away or even coordinated a time that we were all free.

When we got home, I called Addie back.

'Did you get his permission?' she chuckled, without saying hello again.

'Yeah alright, very funny. Look, Mark wasn't given the promotion and he's pretty upset. So upset, he isn't at work today!'

'Oh, I'm sorry, that sucks. Does that mean you can't come?'

'No, I'll be there. I'm hoping he goes to the bachelor party, he really needs to get out.'

'Well, tell him that Dan will be there as well, and he doesn't know many people going. Make sure you book your half-day leave and I'll come and pick you up at around 1pm!'

'Perfect, thanks, Ads! Love you.' I hung up the phone.

'And I love you,' Mark said to me.

'Adeline wanted me to tell you that Dan will be at the bachelor party, and he doesn't really know anyone either so she would love it if you went.' He nodded.

It was back to silence, neither of us sure what to say next. *It hasn't always been like this ... but when did it become like this?*

10

Bachelorette

Having Mark home for a few days wasn't as exciting as I imagined it would be. He seemed withdrawn and cold, despite how much I tried. I was hoping we could go for a walk, see a film or have a romantic dinner, maybe at some point even have sex.

One thing became clear to me, though: Mark had changed. Or I had changed. Or I guess we had both changed. His obsession with the promotion had taken all the fun and joy out of our relationship, and as a result, our intimacy felt non-existent. It felt weird in the house, and I began counting down for the girls' weekend. *Maybe the time away will be good for us?*

'Where're you going?' he asked on Friday as I walked through the front door at noon.

'To Niagara for Eva's bachelorette party, remember? I only had a half-day at work.' I wondered if he had really forgotten.

'Ohh, that's right!'

'Are you going to the bachelor party tomorrow night? Dan is counting on you!' I told him, wanting to get him out of the house for a little while.

'I'm not sure, I haven't really thought about it.'

'Well, I gave Adeline your number so that Dan could call you. I hope that's okay. I think getting out of the house and spending some time with friends would be good for you!'

'They aren't really my friends,' he said, with what I think was sarcasm in his voice.

'Well, they will all be at our wedding one day, so maybe you should take the time to get to know them.' Mark didn't say much to that, which offended me slightly. *Does he not want to marry me?* Mark and I had never spoken much of marriage before, but after so many years together I assumed it would happen when he felt ready. I thought it would be our next step together.

'I'll see you on Sunday night,' I said, kissing him on the lips, trying to be sexy, 'you know, I don't mind being a little late …'

'Is that so?' he said, grabbing a hold of my shoulders and twisting me to point me in the direction of the door.

'Fine!' I said, rolling my eyes and trying to laugh it off once more, even though it hurt that little more each time. The real part of me wanted him to rip my clothes off and make me late. Instead, he helped me put my coat on and ushered me to the door as Adeline honked her car horn.

'Well, enjoy the weekend without me, it will be the last, I'm sure!' I said, kissing him on the cheek.

'What do you mean?' he asked, looking confused.

'I assume you'll be back at work next week – you've already taken a week off?'

'Maybe,' he replied. I heard Adeline yell from the car, which was my cue to kiss him once more and head out the door. As I got in the car, my phone pinged with an email.

Hi Kate,

I trust you're well.

We haven't spoken for a while and saw this deal that had me thinking of

you. It's a trip to Edinburgh with a stopover in Iceland.

It's a great deal, and of course, plenty more where that came from. Have a lovely weekend, and I hope to hear from you soon!

Warm regards,

Jenny

It felt like a lifetime ago that I met that bubbly backpacker and stumbled into Jenny's office. *I can't believe I still haven't even told Mark about it.*

'Get off your phone!' yelled Ads from the driver's seat.

'I am, I am! Let's go!' I screamed back at her, closing down the email and putting my phone into my purse.

'Why aren't I in the front seat? I'm the BACHELORETTE!' Eva said from the back seat.

'Eva, you know you will fall asleep after an hour. I'm in for the long haul!' I joked with her. Adeline made two more stops to pick up Casey and Elise, and then, we were off.

It was a long drive, about seven hours to get to the Canadian border, but everyone was asleep within the hour. Only Adeline and I remained awake.

'So, what happened with Mark?' she asked me.

'Oh, he didn't get the promotion. But he's been home all week, Ad, it's been so weird having him around the house all the time. What's weirder is that he's been home, but we still haven't had sex, every time I try he says he is stressed about what happened with work.'

'Maybe he is?' she said, trying not to be biased.

'But shouldn't that help with stress? I thought sex de-stressed people?' I said, trying to recall an Instagram post I must have learned this educational content from.

'Did you tell him Dan will call him?'

'Yeah, I did. I hope he goes tomorrow night. I think he really needs to have some fun. Urgh. So do I!'

'I'm glad you came,' Adeline said to me, turning and playfully poking me.

'How're you and Dan?' I asked.

'We're good, he keeps bringing up kids, but I told him not until we're married.'

'Ooooo, so do you think there might be a ring on there soon?' I asked, smiling.

'I hope so, I told my family and friends what I like, I've even sent him photos. I'm pretty sure he knows.'

'That's so sweet, I'm happy for you.'

'Have you and Mark spoken about it?'

'We haven't. I made a little comment about it, but he never responded, and honestly, with him and work, and not wanting to travel and us not having any sex, who even knows what will happen?'

'Not wanting to travel?'

'Urgh. Don't get me started. He kept saying no to travel because of the promotion, and then after he didn't get the promotion, he said he had to work harder – but who knows. I think I have to bite the bullet and go by myself.'

'Have you had a proper conversation with him? Like, proper-proper?'

'We kind of did, and he did say I should go without him.'

'By yourself?' She turned to look at me, scrunching her nose and forehead up.

'I know. I'll talk to him.' We continued filling each other in about what had happened over the last few months. Every so often, one of the girls in the back seat would pipe up and ask a question or put her two cents in and then drift off again. It felt so nice to spend time with Adeline that I was sad when we had finally arrived in Niagara. We woke the girls up and Eva went to check us all in.

'I've really missed you,' I said to Adeline.

'You know I'm always here for you. I didn't know any of this was happening between you and Mark, and I'm sorry I haven't been there – life has been so busy.'

'Oh, I know. Sometimes it's easier to pretend like everything is fine as well, you know?'

'I do, but if you keep pretending then you're going to regret it five, ten, twenty years from now. I don't want that for you.' I didn't know what to say, but thanks to Eva, I didn't have to say anything.

'Okay, girls, room 1203.' She led the way and we all followed like excitable girls on a school trip, cheering and chatting away, the mood heightening with the fresh air. Adeline and I knew it was time to park the conversation. Right now, our only priority was Eva.

11

Party

Our Friday night was a relaxed affair, mostly due to the long car journey and desperate need to catch up on each other's lives. We took photos, drank champagne and pampered ourselves. There were different kinds of face masks, platters of food, and it wouldn't have been complete without some old-school nineties' music – the music that took us back to high school and a time of no responsibilities. The songs that, even if we didn't listen to them for years, we would remember every single word, like smells that bring back fond memories. We didn't think about how the late night and alcohol was going to make us feel the next day.

'ALLLRRIIGHHTT, LADIESSSS! WAKE UP!'

We were all woken by Adeline banging pots and pans together, like a child wanting to wake their parent up on some cheesy rom-com.

'Are you serious?' I asked. She was walking around the penthouse banging and shaking anyone's feet she could get her cold hands on. A few other girls arrived that morning and were in the kitchen making mimosas to start the day, multiple voices wafting into the bedroom.

'We have to be at the front of the hotel by 11am for the wine tour, ladies.'

'It's 7am right now though?' Adeline was going to tell me something as Eva's mother walked in.

'Is everyone up, Adeline? It's time for breakfast, ladies!' Eva's mom said. Adeline looked at me and smirked, holding pegs and paper ready to distribute. Reluctantly, I got out of bed to get ready as I overheard her explain the rules.

'If anyone says a man's name – Dan, Scott, Blake etc. – you take their peg. The person at the end of the wine tour that has the most pegs will win a prize. The paper is for each game, and you aren't allowed on the wine tour unless you have completed all of them and have a score recorded.' *What a great way to get everyone participating!*

I got ready and joined everyone in the main room, picking up my pegs and paper, following along as best I could.

On the main table, draped in a white floral-embossed cloth, there was a delicious spread of fruit salad, waffles, cakes, muffins, eggs and yoghurt. Everyone ate while they played games, stopping to take photos of the half-naked 4D cut-out of the groom. The other games were set up in different areas of the penthouse from pin the penis, penis darts and a photo station with the bachelorette. I walked over to the kitchen counter and handed out mimosas to everyone while sipping on my own.

'Kaaaattee! How are you?' I turned around to see an old friend; a girl I always see at Eva's get-togethers but never catch up with outside of them.

'Hi, Sam. I'm good, how are you?'

'I'm fabulous. Lucas and I are engaged!' she squealed with excitement, moving her hand around in the light, trying to show off the sparkle.

'Congratulations!' I inwardly cringed.

'What about you and Mark – I never see him, how is he?'

'He's good, always working, you know, it can be a bit intense some-times!' I said to her – it wasn't a complete lie.

'You guys have been together for what, ten years or something now? Is he going to propose any time soon?'

'It's been eight, and we haven't really spoken about it, just kind of going with the flow,' I told her, probably not sounding very confident in my response. I didn't want to talk about relationships, or engagements, or weddings, or babies. *Why doesn't anyone talk about their work, or how their family are, or their next travel plans or whatever goals they have?*

'Well, *tick-tock, tick-tock!*' she said, playfully nudging me. I played along.

'I'm going to need another mimosa while I finish getting ready, will chat to you after,' I lied, hoping to never cross paths with her and her shiny ring again.

The music was different to last night; it was high-vibe Top 40 music, mostly pop and EDM. Laughter had consumed the room; phones were everywhere taking photos and videos. On our way to the wine tour, I mastered the art of surface-level responses and subtly retreating every time that menial topic arose again. I didn't quite understand why engagements, marriage and babies – in that order – felt like everyone's end goals. It bothered me that it's all anyone knew what to talk about. I was somewhat glad, and amused, that after a few more pinots and chardonnays, after many had left, everyone began discussing their sex life.

'I hope it's not true what they say about no sex after you are married,' Eva was saying over dinner, a slight slur in her words.

'Don't worry too much about after marriage, it happened for us after the kids! They ruin everything,' said one of her friends that I met in the bathroom. She had spilt an entire bottle on herself, rinsed the bottom half of her dress and attempted to dry it in under the hand dryer.

'I think it gets better, Darren and I still do it like we first met, it's like the longer we are together, the more comfortable we are experimenting with new things,' said another girl. At that moment, Adeline pointed at the girl's peg, adding it to all the ones she had collected, winning the game without anyone caring anymore.

'Well, I barely get it now as it is, and we aren't married or have kids. It couldn't get any worse if we were!' I said, to my own surprise, the last pinot taking over and likely matching Eva's slur. A moment after I said it, all the girls' eyes were glued on me, and I realised I should have kept my mouth shut.

'Why, what's happened?' they all chimed in together, curiously prodding.

'I don't know, he said it's the job thing, but I tried the other day and he said no. He keeps saying no. We haven't done it since … since … I don't know, maybe a couple of months now … not that I'm counting … it's actually probably even longer.' I rolled my eyes and took another sip of that sweet, sweet, red liquid courage that was full of tannins and a hint of cocoa and deep berries.

'Do you think he's … gay?' said one girl that I hadn't been introduced to yet.

'Where IS he getting it from, then?' another chimed in.

'Well, I don't think so,' I responded, hesitant and unsure.

'Darren loves it when I dress up for him, maybe try that?'

The unsolicited advice poured in, pushing a seed of doubt further.

Thinking back to our relationship, Mark had never acted that way before, and the thought of bringing it up again made me feel uncomfortable, but I knew, if the dry spell continued, I would have to. Adeline was sitting next to me, and as all the girls moved onto the next topic seamlessly, she turned to me in genuine concern.

'Are you alright?' she whispered, angling her body toward me, gesturing a private conversation now. She put her hand on my right leg and squeezed, an act of comfort.

'Yeah, I'm okay. I hope that Mark and I will be, though.'

'You will be. Talk to him. Maybe a weekend away? A date night with some wine?' I didn't say anything, instead pursed my lips together and nodded. She picked up her drink and we clinked our glasses together, watching the wine swish from side to side before entering our mouths one more time.

The bartender placed two tequila shots in front of us, like a sign from the universe to let go, to have some fun.

'Last one for me,' said Adeline, 'I have to drive all day tomorrow!' We raised our shot glasses together and knocked them back, allowing the night to continue without any reference to marriage, babies and men. Bliss! We put our worries aside and focused on being present, enjoying each other's company just like old times.

12

Talk

Mark and I kept our distance from each other over the next few days; I didn't feel the urge to keep trying and he didn't seem to want to either, a mix of disappointment my end after he told me he didn't go to the bachelor party and the seeds planted from the bachelorette's.

'How was your day?' he asked unusually cheerfully one evening, as I walked into the kitchen after work.

'Fine. Eileen forgot I had booked leave for the wedding, so that was a fun conversation.' I rolled my eyes. 'And I received an email from a travel agency with some potential deals for my trip.' I waited for a reaction, watching him sauté the chicken. 'Have you had any other thoughts about going away?' I noticed he hesitated, his arm stopped moving – just for a moment – then continued.

'I'm not sure, I really don't think it's good timing, babe.'

I took a deep breath and nodded, removing my coat and draping it over the dining room table.

'Red?' he asked. I nodded. *Is he trying to change the subject?* It was silent as he poured the wine and we both took a sip. It was a long silence; I decided to break it.

'I feel like we've lost our connection. I was with all these women talking about their amazing sex lives, their engagements, wedding plans and babies. I feel like we've lost it, we've lost our spark, and we aren't doing anything to find it again.' Mark was silent, thinking, and continued cooking.

'I know. I'm sorry about the last couple months. I'll work on it.'

'You say that, but what about marriage? Kids? We don't speak about any of that.'

'What about it? I'm not ready for that! *We're* not ready for that.'

'We're in our thirties now, Mark. All of our friends are getting engaged and starting to settle down. My biological clock is ticking too.' I heard the girl echo from the bachelorette's – *tick-tock, tick-tock.*

'I don't know if I even want to get married,' he finally said.

My heart beat faster, it felt like it was burning. *Wait, what?! He doesn't know if he wants to get married?*

'Since when?' I asked, confused. *Mark has never mentioned this before!*

'I never said I wanted to get married.'

'You never said that you explicitly didn't. What about kids?' I asked, wondering if I even knew him at all.

'I don't know,' he said quietly, almost under his breath. He wasn't looking at me.

'Is it you don't want to get married and have children with *me,* or you generally don't want to get married and have children *at all?*'

'I don't know – I don't know, Katie!' he responded, raising his voice in frustration. I stormed out of the kitchen and into the bedroom, my head buried in my hands, crying. *Was this a waste of eight years? Have I always known this deep down inside?* I could hear Mark coming into the room, then I could feel him sitting on the bed next to me.

'Is this why you want me to go travelling alone? Can you even see a future together for us?'

'Of course I can. We have so much history. I don't know if I want to get married or have children, though. It's a big commitment. Our life is so perfect the way it is.'

Perfect?

'Why is this the first time you've said this to me?'

'I guess I was scared of looking at the bigger picture. The idea of planning a future together … I'm not ready for it. I don't know if I will ever be ready for it.'

'So, you thought you would string me along to see what would happen, and what – hoped I would never bring it up?' A part of me wished we had never gotten into this tonight; it would've been easier pretending nothing was wrong and to go about our days.

'You know it's not like that,' he said, but I didn't believe him.

'Maybe we need some time apart,' I said quietly, not fully comprehending where this left us.

'What do you mean?'

'I can go and stay at Mom's for a while. Maybe we both need to figure out what we want.'

'Do you really think that's a good idea?'

'I do.'

'Let's take a breather. I'll sleep on the couch tonight, okay? Let's not make any irrational decisions right now. I've nearly finished dinner – c'mon,' he said, leaving the room. I didn't want to eat dinner and pretend everything was okay. I got up and started packing instead, watching my tears drip onto the clothes I was folding. I could hear Mark taking the plates out, the ceramic moving from benchtop to table, the clinking of the cutlery. I picked up the phone and called Mom.

'Chookie? It's late, is everything okay?'

'Not exactly. Mark and I are going to spend some time apart. I need a place to stay. Is anyone staying at the Brooklyn house?' I asked.

'Oh, love, I'm so sorry. You can stay as long as you like.'

'Thanks, I'm calling in sick tomorrow.'

'I can pick you up now if you want?' she kindly offered.

'No, it's fine. I'm really tired, and it's getting late. Mark said he would sleep on the couch.'

'Are you sure you're okay?' she asked, I could hear the sadness in her voice.

'I'll be fine, Mom. I'm okay.'

'Everything will work out, chooks.'

'I know, Mom. I'll see you tomorrow.' As I continued to pack my things, I went over and over our conversation and tried to take it all in. *How, in eight years, could he have only said this to me now? When did we stop sharing our goals and dreams? When did we drift so far apart from each other?*

13

Move

I woke up at 7:59am; a minute before my alarm went off. It took me a moment for my eyes to adjust to the sunlight coming in through the curtains. I felt like I'd been struck down with a cold – my whole body ached, my eyes felt puffy, my sinuses were sore and my head was spinning. *Did last night really happen?* Hoping it was a dream until I saw my half-packed suitcase on the floor.

'Katelyn? Are you okay?' the receptionist asked.

'I won't be in today, Tara.'

'No problem, rest up. I'll let Eileen know.'

I lay in bed and watched the beams of light bounce off the walls. Then the phone rang: it was Mom.

'Kate, it's 8am, I haven't heard from you? Have you and Mark sorted things out?'

'No. Come over at noon?' She agreed and we hung up.

I found it weird that I hadn't heard Mark get ready. *Had he come into the room? Had he left already? Is he still in the lounge?* I didn't know what to do, safely staying in bed with Luna by my feet. Silence. The house felt empty. When I went into the living room, there was no briefcase, no mobile and no shoes. He'd left. I started crying again. The blanket he used was still draped over the seats, and I found myself laying in it, wrapped up in it almost pretending he stayed home to hold me.

'Are you coming with me?' I asked Luna, who followed me so obediently. 'Maybe if we ask Grandma nicely? You can't be here home alone.' Mom wouldn't have let her stay though; she wasn't fond of dogs in the house.

I continued packing a few bits and pieces before having a shower. I felt I needed to take enough to show Mark I was serious, but enough to come back when we worked things out. *Will we work things out? Is it too late for that?*

The doorbell rang and I opened the door.

'Oh dear,' said Mom, looking at me with pity in her eyes.

'I don't know what happened. He told me he didn't want to get married and have kids.' I felt like I was going to cry, but nothing would come out anymore.

'You guys will work things out,' she said. I knew there was more she wanted to say but it wasn't the right time. She walked me around the apartment and asked if I needed anything.

'I'm taking the coffee machine,' I said as I unplugged it.

'Kate, there's one in Brooklyn.'

'No, I bought this one and I'm taking it. If he doesn't want marriage and kids, he sure as hell can't have my coffee machine.' Mom chuckled, not realising how serious I was being.

I glared, trying to juggle everything in my arms.

'What about this one?' She was pointing at Luna, who was sitting by the front door ready to come. Without even responding, she picked Luna up and took her to the car.

I looked at our apartment, thinking back to when we first moved in together and how happy we were. *This is it.* Locking the door behind me, I wondered when I would next be back.

The drive to Brooklyn was silent, it felt like a blur. I didn't even realise we had pulled into the driveway; it was only the slamming of the car door when Mom got out that brought me back to reality. It felt strange to be back at this house again, my childhood home. This was American suburbia at its finest. The green lawns were perfectly manicured, and a little white picket fence separated each property. No city hustle-bustle here, but I liked it.

'Lindelle, is that little Katy-Kat?' Mom looked over and waved at the neighbour watering her garden: an old European woman, a slight hunch in her back.

'It sure is. She isn't so little anymore, though, is she?' I stared at her blankly but smiled to be polite. *Katy-Kat? No-one ever calls me Katy-Kat.*

'Who was that?' I asked Mom when we were inside, knowing the neighbour wouldn't hear me.

'You don't remember Aunty Rita? She used to look after you as a kid,' she said, turning the kettle on. I shook my head, my attention taken by the renovated kitchen much different from what I remembered.

'Gosh, it feels like I haven't been here in years!' I told Mom.

'You haven't,' she said shortly. It was true. I moved out long before Mom did. Mom bought this house herself after she left Dad, and we grew up in it. Once Mom and Derrick moved upstate, there was no reason to visit the family home. Mom rented it out through Airbnb throughout the year and kept all our things locked in some of the closets.

'Why did you keep it?' I asked, getting the key from her so I could look through my boxes.

'Maybe for reasons like this,' she said, smiling at me. 'I can't seem to let it go.'

I opened the box and my eyes welled up with tears once more, but not from heartache this time.

'Oh my god. Do you remember this?' I asked her, dusting off an old DSLR camera. It was front and centre in the box.

'That thing was glued to you, how could I forget it?' she laughed, handing me a cup of tea.

'You kept it?'

'I wasn't going to throw out something so special to you. I hoped the two of you would be reunited one day.'

Mom watched as I blew off the dust and wiped the lens with my shirt. When I looked up, I saw it wasn't only my eyes that were teary – hers were too.

'What?' I asked, trying not to cry with all the emotions I was feeling.

'That was the same smile you had when I first gave it to you. You were talented, you know?' I didn't know what to say to her, so I didn't say anything and kept digging through the box instead to find old clothes I used to wear and books from high school.

'Gosh, what was I thinking?!' I asked, taking out a floral-print summer dress.

'I thought you dressed very funky.'

I looked at her and laughed. *Funky?* 'Please, I would have looked like a hippie in this!'

Mom didn't say anything to that, even though I could tell she wanted to.

'I'm going to pop out to pick up some food. There isn't anything to eat here. I'll spend the night too, it's too far to drive home for me tonight.'

'Thanks, Mom.' I knew she was staying because she didn't want me home alone. She had driven at night multiple times after visiting us in Manhattan.

When she was gone, I took off my black pants and beige blouse, now with a dark circular stain from the dust, and put on the floral hippie dress. It fit. It used to be my favourite until Mark once said I looked like a Romanian gypsy. I was surprised it still fit after all these years; feeling the way the straps sat loosely on my shoulders and the drawstring sat perfectly on my waist. Oh, and the hidden pockets. Loved the pockets.

I swirled in the lounge, and even though the musky scent of it was now wafting through the room, I didn't mind.

What else is in the box? Right at the bottom there was a photo album with some of the photos I had taken with the camera, including the very first photo I'd taken of Mark the night we met at the Irish bar. *What is he doing right now? Is he thinking about me? Is he missing me?* I put my clothes back on before Mom got home, and sat on the old, sunken couch that had been there my whole life. *Is it full circle, and now I'm starting a new chapter?* I remembered where Mom hid the gin and poured myself one before settling down to look through the old pictures. Many, many memories. The family. The girls. Mark.

'Mom?' I yelled as I heard the front door open.

The smell of the finest Brooklyn pepperoni pizza followed her through the doorway. She didn't answer me, and instead put the pizza and wine on the coffee table. 'I think it's about time I started taking pictures again!' Mom didn't say anything again; she just poured a glass of wine for us and held it up.

'Chook, that's the best thing I've heard all week!'

14

Brooklyn

My puffy eyes and tired face made for an excellent cover story when I went back to work. I didn't want to tell anyone what Mark and I were going through … *Who even knows what we are going through? And why hasn't he called yet?* Every time I had a notification on my phone, I hoped it was him. It never was.

The days felt like years, and then weeks passed which felt like a decade, but gradually things got easier and more bearable. I started to think less about Mark and used the long evenings and weekends to rediscover my hometown. Brooklyn had always held a place in my heart, even though I had moved to Manhattan. Mark never liked it though; he didn't like the street vibe and hated the thought of me growing up in the rougher part of the city.

'Why live there when you can afford not to?' he once asked me when we were looking for a place to live. I had never really thought twice about it – in fact, I agreed with him. Living in Manhattan was never a concern of mine, never a place I really thought about moving to until I met Mark. *Was moving to Manhattan even what I wanted to do?* I used to sit at Fort Greene Park for hours, watching all the different characters go by, and I was looking forward to doing that again.

'Is everything okay, Katelyn?' Eileen called out just as I was about to walk out the door my first day back in the office.

'Yeah, why?' I asked her, wondering if Mark had called to tell her. *Would he do that?*

'You haven't been yourself these last few days.'

'Oh … it's been a few weeks since you last said that. Has something been wrong with my work?'

'No, it's not your work, that's been fine. It's you. *You* are the one I'm worried about.' I could feel my eyes fill, a stinging sensation in my sinuses as I pushed it away. *Please don't say his name. Please don't say his name.*

'Thanks, but I'm fine. Have a good weekend, Eileen,' I quickly said, forcing a smile and leaving the office before she saw me break down into tears. I had an urge to run, and I did. The cool air dried my eyes and my heart beat faster, blood rushing through my body. My chest felt tight quickly; thankfully, I needed to stop for a crowd of tourists. *Don't be ridiculous, Katelyn. This is Manhattan and it's rush hour, it's no time to run. Walk. Breathe. Walk. Breathe.* I put my sunglasses on, using them like an invisibility cloak, walking instinctively toward the wrong train that would no longer take me in the direction of my home. I was already on the carriage when I realised. *Maybe I should go to our house? Maybe I should talk to Mark?* My ego didn't allow me to. Instead, I walked off, mournfully, and made my way to Park Slope, Brooklyn.

Ring ring ring ring. My phone. It was Adeline. Groan. I hadn't told her yet.

'Katie!' said the chirpy, high-pitched voice of my best friend that didn't know what I had been going through yet.

'What are you doing?' I asked.

'Just leaving work now, why?'

'Come over and share a bottle of red with me, I'm going to order a pizza on my way home too?'

'Everything okay?'

'I need a yes or no, Ads!'

'I'll leave in twenty, I'm just …'

'And I'm living at Mom's at the moment, so go there, in Brooklyn.'

'Wait, what?' There was a moment of silence while she processed what I was trying to tell her. 'Leaving now, babe.' She hung up the phone, and I was glad that she would arrive at the same time as me, I'd had enough of being in that house alone.

When I got off the subway, I saw another familiar face.

'Heyyy!' I yelled out as loudly as I could, waving my hand and running across the road trying to avoid the cars. The girl looked up, and slowly, realising we had met before, started smiling and walking towards me. 'Felicity, right?'

'Katelyn! Hi, how are you?' She left the group of friends she was standing with and reached out to give me a hug, I felt a wave of warm energy rush through me.

'Yeah, I'm good. Just staying at my mom's house at the moment. What are you doing in Brooklyn?'

'Well, I hear they have the best pizzas, so a bunch of us from the hostel decided to judge for ourselves.'

'And?' I asked her, raising my eyebrows, expecting a good result.

'Amazing!' she said, laughing while rubbing her belly. 'Probably couldn't live here for that reason, these pants wouldn't fit!' I laughed too. It was nice to laugh with someone again.

'Are you travelling around New York?' I asked her, curious to know more of her story.

'Yes, I've been backpacking around North America for about three months now.'

'Three months?! Wow. How do you do that? What about work?'

'I saved a lot before I left, but I figure we need to work until we're sixty. Why not enjoy life while we can?' Her face lit up, so confident with her choice. I could feel how inspired she was, how alive she was, 'Were you born here?'

'I was, here in Park Slope actually, I haven't really left New York.'

'Well, you should. New York is amazing but it's still only a small part of the world!' I knew she was right.

'C'mon, Felicity!' someone was yelling in the distance. Felicity looked over at the group – guys and girls, all looking to be in their early twenties.

'I have to go. We're meeting someone soon, but add me on Facebook. Felicity Williams. Let's stay in touch.' She hugged me once more and walked off quickly to catch up with her friends, waving as she disappeared around the corner.

Felicity Williams. I typed it into Facebook and Instagram as I ordered my pizza.

'I thought you were never coming back!' Gianni handed over the pizza, winking at me. Gianni had seen me grow up; I even did some work at his shop for extra cash in my teens. 'It's nice to see your smile around here again.' It seemed strange that so many people in this neighbourhood remembered me and were still there after so many years. I had been in Manhattan for five years now, and other than Salvatore at the pizza joint, nobody knew who I was. Nobody cared who I was. *Maybe that is the problem? Maybe I'm missing a sense of community?*

Felicity Williams. Her pages were public. I scrolled through photos and photos of mountains, oceans, people and landmarks. It was inspiring. Her face felt like a call to action.

Hi Jenny,

Sorry for the late reply, a lot's been going on.

That holiday sounds perfect and I'd like to book it in for next month.

Cheers,

Katelyn

Can I do that? Can I quit my job? Can I go away for three months? Can I go alone? What about Mark? What about our Luna? I didn't feel scared though – I felt excited.

How much notice do I need to give at work? Where do I go? Can I really afford this? As I got home and took my coat off, a coloured piece of card came out as well. It read:

A comfort zone is a beautiful place, but nothing ever grows there. – Gina Milicia

The longer I stared at it, the more obvious a little love heart was at the bottom left-hand corner with the initials FW. Felicity? It made me smile – it was a call to action, perfectly timed with Adeline's arrival.

'You, have a lot to tell me, miss!' she said, walking in and hugging me, a serious look on her face, a bottle of red wine in hand.

'Well, let me start with … I think I'm going to quit my job and go travelling for a few months!' I paused to wait for a reaction. Adeline looked at me stunned.

'You're kidding, right?'

'Nope, Mark and I have taken a break and he hasn't called me in a few weeks. I bumped into this backpacker again, and honestly, I think it's exactly what I need. I need to get away and find myself again. I don't know who I am anymore.' Adeline began smiling, a grin so big more gum than usual was showing.

'What?' I asked her, confused.

'You really have lost it!' She walked over to the ugly brown couch we used to play games on as kids and picked up the floral dress that I hadn't put back in the box.

'You loved this thing,' she said, feeling nostalgic.

'I know, look behind you.' I pointed behind her, nodding towards the table where my camera had been sitting.

'No way! Your mom kept it?' I nodded slowly, my eyebrows raised, expressing to her how surprised I was too.

'Kate, I think you should go!'

'No way, are you serious?'

'Honestly, you have been talking about travelling for as long as I've known you. I remember how upset you were when Mark talked you into that shitty all-inclusive resort for your anniversary, and how devastated you were that he wouldn't leave the resort. You need to do this!' I couldn't fault Adeline as a friend, she knew me the best out of anyone in this world, even though we never saw each other like we used to.

'Well, let's get to it, then!' she said, finding two wine glasses, looking as at home as I did.

'To what?' I asked her, not sure what she was referring to.

'Let's type your resignation letter and plan your adventure!' she yelled from the kitchen, but as I slowly walked toward her, she must have realised I wasn't taking her seriously. She looked me in the eye and said with complete conviction, 'If you want to do this, do it!' And just like that, I knew I was about to embark on an adventure.

15

Resignation

Before I knew it, I was walking into work with my resignation letter in hand – my trembling hand – ready to give it to Eileen at the end of the day. At first, I felt confident and empowered. As the day dragged on, I was growing more and more anxious by the minute. I struggled to focus on work and couldn't stomach lunch, not to mention obsessing over the time. I had to keep looking through Felicity's photos to remind myself that it was all going to be worth it.

When it finally hit 5pm I headed straight for Eileen. I'd already packed my bag and put on my jacket so I could make a quick exit, small beads of sweat around my lip and chin.

'Hi, Eileen,' I acted casual even though my heart felt like it was beating out of my chest. Eileen stopped what she was doing and looked up at me; she could tell something was up.

'Katelyn. Everything alright?' she asked.

'Yes, it is. I'm. Um. I'm here to give you my four weeks' notice.'

'Excuse me?' she asked after a moment of silence. I walked to her desk, and as the paper shook in my hands, handed it to her.

'I appreciate the opportunities you've given me here, however, I think it's time I move on.'

'Where are you going?'

'I want to travel, and as you reminded me, policy states I only have two weeks leave and am not entitled to any more than that, so unfortunately I don't have any other choice.' I was picking my cuticles nervously, shifting weight between each heel, unable to remain still.

'How long are you going away for?' she asked me.

'I don't know, probably a few months.'

'And … Mark?' she continued prodding.

'I'm not sure, but either way, I need to do this.'

'You're sure about this?' Eileen asked, leaning forward on her desk, her elbows pressing into it.

'No, I'm not. I only know I need to make some sort of life change.' Eileen sat quietly staring at the folded A4 paper.

'You know how hard it is to get a job out there at the moment, don't you?'

'I know, but I've realised there is never going to be a perfect time.'

'Are you sure everything is alright, Katelyn? Do you want to sleep on this a few more days?' Eileen sounded sincere in her questions, which I didn't think was possible. She always made me feel like I was just another employee.

'I'm sure it will be.' She nodded her head as to drop the interrogation and smiled at me, the corner of her mouth ever so slightly arching upward, a sight rarely seen. We didn't need to say more than that. As I walked out, it felt like the weight of the world had lifted off my shoulders. I didn't feel as sad as I thought I would, in fact, quite the opposite. I felt good. I felt confident. I felt inspired. I texted Adeline it was over and then called Mom.

'Hey, Mom, how are you?'

'I'm good, love, how are you? You sound chirpy? How is everything in Brooklyn?'

'Good, just on my way there now … I won't be staying there too much longer, another month maybe.'

'Oh! You and Mark are back together?'

'No, we aren't. I handed my resignation in, and I've decided to go travelling.'

'Huh? Wait. What? Where?' she was as surprised as Eileen.

'I spoke to an agent a while ago on a whim and we've been in touch quite a bit. She's been sending me incredible package deals. Since Mark and I aren't together anymore, I figured I might as well just go for it. I need to do this.'

'I know you do, sweetheart.' I knew a part of her wanted to talk me out of it, but she also knew I needed to get away.

'I'd really like to go to Scotland and visit Patrick and the rest of the family. What do you think?' Mom went silent; I wondered what she was thinking. *Maybe she doesn't want me to meet him?*

'I think that's a wonderful idea, Katie. His daughter Alice is about your age, I think – you should get in touch with her.'

'Do you want to come with me?'

'Thanks, darling, but no, too much time has passed. I couldn't see him now. We've both moved on.'

'I'm glad you approve, Mom. And … would you be open to taking care of Luna? Mark is not home enough.'

'Let me talk to Derrick and I'll email you all the details I have, okay?' I could hear a slight cracking in her voice. *Is it the line? Or is she upset?*

'I love you,' I said, hoping she'd heard me before hanging up. It was only a few moments after I had walked through the front door that Mom sent through Patrick's and Alice's email along with, Derrick said it was fine, he will put up a fence for Loons. As quick as I received the email, I needed to send one:

Dear Alice,

Hope all is well with you!

I'm your long-lost cousin living in New York, Lindelle's daughter (your dad will know her). I'm planning a trip to Scotland and would love to meet with you and Uncle Patrick, and anyone else that I may be related to that I don't know about!

Let me know if you'd be free around mid-November, I haven't finalised dates yet but will let you know when I do.

Warm regards,

Katelyn

I pressed send, wondering what she would think receiving an email like that from a woman she had never met before. It was 11am in Scotland. *Will she read it straight away? Will she respond today? Will she respond at all? Will she just delete it? Has Patrick told her about my mom?* I didn't want to keep thinking about it and found the last few emails with Jenny instead. We had emailed back and forth for a few days with possible travel routes, and finally settled on Iceland, Scotland and Hawaii before heading back to New York, all with flexible flight dates in case I decided to stay somewhere longer or shorter.

It felt easy organising it with Jenny, but reading through the itinerary and knowing I would be unemployed and leaving New York by myself was starting to scare me. *Can I really travel alone? Is it really the end of Mark and me?* It made me feel nervous, and before imploding with anxiety, I received an email. And butterflies set in instead.

Hi Katelyn,

It's so lovely to hear from you, I never thought in a million years I would! And of course – Dad and I would love to have you here. Let us know the dates. Add me on Facebook and Instagram so I can follow your travels as well. We have a guest room that you can use for however long you fancy. I'm about to go into a meeting, but we should organise a call soon. Thanks for getting in touch; I'm very excited to meet you!

Love, Alice

I couldn't stop smiling. *Okay, that's one question down … only a million more to go!*

Sheleila D'Paiva

16

Transition

Mark and I hadn't spoken for weeks since I left; I had been making do with the clothes I had packed and what I found in the boxes. I checked his social media when I first woke every morning – never anything new. It took all my self-control not to call him, but I wanted to tell him about my trip. It bothered me. I questioned his love for me, I questioned his love for Luna. What time did, though, was allow me to realise I couldn't place all the blame on him as much as I wanted to. I could call. I could have brought up marriage and kids earlier. I realised I took a back seat to my own life.

The Saturday after putting in my resignation, I finally called him. My finger hovered over the red hang-up button for a second, but I resisted and let it ring.

'Katelyn?' he answered. Urgh. He picked up.

'Hi, Mark, I called to see when I could come by and pick up the rest of my things?' I tried to sound diplomatic, but I'm sure it came across rude and blunt. *Is that why he didn't call? He knew at some point I would have to get my things?*

'Yeah sure, when?' Even his response triggered me. *That's all he wants to say? Even though that's all I wanted to say.*

'Well, I'm on my way back home now, I can get an Uber over?' I suggested.

'Yeah sure, I guess that's fine. I haven't got much planned for today, so ...'

'Okay great. See you around four? Bye,' and without a response, I disconnected the line. For a moment, it felt good to have the last word and show him I was perfectly fine without him, but the moments following made me feel sad. It didn't feel like I had been in a relationship for eight years with this man. We didn't feel like friends. And if I was being honest with myself, I did miss him, and I didn't like the way I handled the conversation – or lack of one. *What if he isn't doing that well?*

Once I reached home, I got ready. I did my hair, my make-up and put on a new outfit that screamed 'new-me' vibes. Then I headed to Mark's place. Our place? *Do I ring the bell? Do I use my key and just walk in?* I decided to be polite and buzzed the door to let Mark know I was there but used my key. The apartment felt empty; it felt cold. It didn't feel like a place I once called home.

'Katie,' Mark said, walking from the kitchen toward me. He reached in for a hug, but I stood limp.

'How are you?'

'I'm good, how are you?' he responded, exchanging surface-level pleasantries.

'I'm fine.' There was an awkward silence while I stood there, looking around at our home. I took a deep breath and sighed, moving past him and toward our bedroom. Mark let me lead, but slowly followed behind.

'Maybe you should give me some space while I do this?' I said to him, looking toward the front door.

'Kate, c'mon ... let's talk about this?'

'I don't think there is anything to talk about, I think your lack of contact over the last month has told me everything I needed to know,' I responded hypocritically, putting things in another suitcase.

'Just like that? After eight years together?'

'Just like that? I haven't heard from you.' I snorted, confused as to why he didn't call me sooner if that's the way he really felt.

'You didn't call me either. And what are you going to do? Go back to living in Brooklyn?'

My heart started beating faster and the hairs on the back of my neck stood up, my hands clamming up. I could feel the heat radiate through my entire body.

'And there it is again, revealing your chauvinistic self.'

'Excuse me?' He sounded confused, or at least surprised I had talked back to him for a change.

'What? You! You and your arrogance! What makes you better than anyone else? Who cares if I live in Brooklyn, it's quite clear you don't mind where I go as long as you get to keep the house,' I said, now raising my voice. 'I can't wait to leave this place!' Mark had never heard me raise my voice before. Complain? Yes. Nag? Yes. Whinge? Yes. Yell? Never. 'I'm done, Mark. I'm finally going travelling. Something I have put off for years because of you.' His face changed.

'What?' he asked me, his voice now soft and calm.

'I've quit my job to go travelling, that's why I need my stuff. I'll pack it in boxes and leave it at Mom's. We will sort the rest out later.'

'Resigned? Are you crazy?'

There was so much frustration in me, so much sadness and disappointment that I didn't want to be polite to him, I didn't want to be kind or considerate. But I also didn't want to regret anything. I took a deep breath and got myself together, sitting down on the bed.

'For what it's worth, Katie, I really miss you. This house isn't a home without you. I didn't call because I didn't know what to say. I buried myself in work and I knew at some point you needed to get your things.'

I fell silent, choosing to think before I spoke first.

'My flights are booked, and I'm not missing them.'

'How long are you gone for?'

'I don't know,' I hesitated for a moment, 'I can't promise you anything, Mark.'

Mark remained silent; I continued packing, slightly more composed but thinking of what he had just said. I strategically packed my clothes, then shoes, then some perfumes.

'I'm sorry for the things I said to you,' he said, sitting on the bed with his body bent forward, chin in hands and elbows on knees. 'I didn't realise how much I missed you, how much I do want you in my life, and if that means marriage and kids, then let's do it.' The comfortable side of me wanted to embrace him, to feel that comfort again, to feel the love, to feel home. The part of me that had begun to flourish over the last few weeks was the current captain of the ship, the side that remembered what he said, the differences that lay between us, and how much we had changed.

'I'm leaving, Mark,' I said, exiting the bedroom.

'Katie?' he called once more, wanting me to turn back to him, but I couldn't. I didn't want him to see the tears running down my face, so I left without looking back.

17

Departure

I waited until the day I left to pick up a few final documents from Jenny. I think a part of me was scared that Mark would come back into my life and I would quickly lose the courage to leave. I saw him a couple of times to pick more things up, but we didn't seem to be able to communicate properly anymore. I didn't even know if I still wanted to work on things, or if I was looking for an excuse not to go. Every part of me was scared to leave New York, not only to travel alone for the first time, but that I was making all the wrong decisions. *Maybe Mark and I are supposed to be together? Maybe I shouldn't have quit my job? Maybe I need to just be satisfied with all that I have here?* That wasn't the only thing on my mind, though. It bothered me there was no contact in-between when I needed to visit. Mark didn't check in when I moved to Brooklyn – on me or our Luna. He only seemed to try and talk when I was making an effort or at the house. I went over it again and again in my mind. So unsure, so confused.

'Are you okay?' I looked up and saw Jenny's face; she had a look of genuine concern.

'I'm nervous. I thought this would be such an exciting moment, but I don't feel excited anymore.' Jenny had no idea what was going on in my personal life, and I didn't want to explain it to a stranger.

'If things are meant to be, they will be, Katelyn.' I looked at her, confused. 'Well, you know, the single ticket, the change of address and emergency contact,' she continued gently. I looked down, embarrassed and ashamed.

'Come and visit me when you're back, okay? I promise you, you will not regret this. You will learn so much about yourself, about the world, and you will surely meet some interesting characters.' I forced an unconvincing smile and took my travel documents from her hand, unable to say anything in case I began to crumble.

As I made my way back to Brooklyn, I reassured myself I had done the right thing, checking Felicity's social media once more to see all the fun she was having. I checked Alice's too, studying her face like I had done multiple times already.

'Where have you been, we need to leave now!' Mom frantically yelled when I walked through the door, all my bags by the doorway. 'Do you want to miss your flight?' *Do I?* Derrick was sitting on the couch watching quietly as Mom paced up and down.

'I thought we were waiting for Adeline?' I asked them, subconsciously trying to delay.

'Adeline said she would meet us there. It's time to go now.' Derrick carried my bags to the car as Mom and I followed.

'I could have taken an Uber, you know?' I said to them, peering out of the window. Mom sat in the back seat with me, holding my hand. I wondered how it felt for a mom to let their child go overseas, unable to watch over or protect them, or be near enough to help if they needed it. She handed me a brown-paper-wrapped box. It was hard and heavy.

'You guys didn't have to get me anything,' I said, slowly unwrapping their gift. As I opened it, my heart felt warm. It was the newest edition Nikon, a camera I'd been thinking about getting before my trip but decided my old one was good enough. 'How did you know?!'

'Well, I walked into the camera store and asked for their best camera,'

Mom responded. Derrick looked over at me from the driver's seat and winked.

'What do you think?' he asked me, his grey moustache moving as he spoke.

'It's beautiful!' I told them. I handed Mom the old one that I was carrying in my backpack, knowing she would put it back in its home – back in one of the old boxes where parts of me were kept. I didn't want to cry again, so I bit my lip and looked out of the window.

Adeline was already waiting by Starbucks when we arrived, her olive skin and perfect long brown hair that was always curled at the bottom. *Gosh, I am going to miss her smile.* She ran up to us and hugged us all, one by one.

'I'm so proud of you, Kate, and I'm so jealous! I must come visit you,' she said.

'Are you sure you don't want come with me now?' I asked her, not joking at all.

'I wish!' is all she said, both of us sharing expressions of excitement and terror.

'Remember, this is all fate, and it's happening for a reason, okay?'

'That's what I keep hearing,' I said, rolling my eyes. I hugged everyone for the last time after checking in my bags, and walked through the gate alone, holding tears back. The vision of the three of them made my heart hurt but beat a little faster.

Doesn't he know I'm leaving today? Has he forgotten? I'm sure he knew, he just chose not to be there, and there was nothing I could do about it. I took a deep breath and let out as much emotion as I silently could. It was time the tears stopped. *I'm here. I'm doing this. It's going to be amazing.* I wasn't sure how much self-talk was needed to believe it, but I continued the self-affirmations, the mantras. And by the time I was seated at the gate, the sadness had stopped and the butterflies I had been longing for had finally returned. The butterflies knew the next stop was Iceland …

18

Quella

I sat by the window inside the terminal and nervously watched the workers in hi-vis on the tarmac do things to the plane; it was such a small plane compared to the others. *How is this measly little plane going to get us to Iceland? What is the likelihood of it crashing? How much turbulence could something that small truly withstand?* It was a terrible rabbit hole to dive into before take-off and I couldn't help but start thinking about the MH370 tragedy. *What if this plane just vanished off the radar, never to be seen again? What if I was the only survivor? Would I even know how to fend for myself? Would I eat the other passengers to stay alive? What are the chances?* The logical side of me knew the chances were pretty low – at least, I hoped the chances were pretty low. The logical side of me also decided it was time to get my mind onto something more constructive, immediately thinking of my brand-new camera.

As I was reading about the different attachments to my Nikon, an earthy voice grabbed my attention. I looked over to see a tall and built woman; she looked European, with dark brown hair and a plumpness to her skin, making her look young. I watched her sit down and ask the elderly gentleman next to her the time, he responded and looked back down at his newspaper, clearly not interested in conversing with her. She turned to the person to the left and asked about their stay in New York; the middle-aged woman, looking tired, smiled and allowed the conversation to continue. It made me think of Felicity, she would have definitely spoken to this woman. As I looked down at the camera manual again, everyone started boarding. I watched as the line got longer and longer, then, as it got shorter and shorter. *This is it.* I took out my boarding pass and passport from my travel wallet and handed it over. *Last chance. Breathe.* I stepped onto the plane, smiling at the attendants that were greeting all the passengers, checking tickets once more. It smelt like disinfectant.

Many had already boarded with their headphones on looking straight ahead, I had to angle my body numerous times, trying not to hit the ones sitting on the aisle seat. Some people were holding up the line as they put their carry-on in the overhead compartment, while many placed them by their feet under the chair in front. I assumed that's why people wanted to get on the plane faster, to get comfortable in their seats earlier. As soon as I sat, I heard that cheerful European voice get closer and closer.

'Howdy!' she said, standing in the aisle facing me, oblivious to the line she was holding up behind her.

'Oh, hi. 14C?' I asked.

'You can bet your bottom dollar, I am! Lucky you!' she laughed heart-ily. The kind of laugh that intuitively made you smile and feel fuzzy inside. Her voice was deep, strong, confident. I didn't know whether it was a good or bad thing that I had to spend the next six hours of my life sitting next to her.

'First time?' she asked.

'Pardon? First time for what?'

'Flying? Iceland? You tell me!'

'Oh, I see,' I laughed awkwardly. 'It's not my first time flying, but it is my first time to Iceland!'

'What makes you want to go there?'

'I don't know – well, my travel agent recommended it, a great stop-over on my way to Scotland, apparently.'

'Ahhh, yes! What are you doing in Scotland?'

'Just meeting some family!' I said, preparing myself for the next question.

'How lovely! Well, it's a pleasure to meet you. I'm Quella!'

'It's nice to meet you too. I'm Katelyn. Is this your first time to Iceland?' I asked her, finally getting my own question in.

'Nope, I was visiting relatives in New York. I work in Reykjavík. I'm one of the lunatics that take people like you out to wait in the cold and see the northern lights!' she laughed.

'Wow, does it ever get old?' I asked her, curious.

'Nope, never. Mother Nature always gives me something different to look at, and sometimes she gives me nothing at all! Which sucks for you guys, but it is what it is.'

'What happens when … nothing happens?'

'Well, a lot of disappointed tourists, that's for sure. It baffles me how they assume they'll see something … It's as if the lights are operated by a magic switch! Where are you staying, anyway?'

'Green Paradise Hotel.'

'Oh nice, have you picked any packages? I hope I didn't talk you out of anything!'

'No, not really. I was just going to wait until I got there to see what my options were.'

'Awesome! Well, let me know if you want some suggestions,' she offered politely.

'I will, thank you!' It was nice speaking to a stranger; I wasn't really used to it, and I did wonder what if she was a kidnapper or human trafficker. Just in case she was, I told her my husband was living in New York and that he was meeting me out there. What I was really saying was 'if you kidnap me, there are people in the world who know I exist, and they will find you'.

A couple hours into the flight, once the food had started coming around, Quella confided in me. She told me about how she once dated an astronomer, and that they both visited Iceland for the first time together. She told me how she completely fell in love with the country, left the astronomer, got a job as a tour guide and has been living there ever since. She flies back to New York a few times a year to see her family.

'Wow. I couldn't imagine doing that, just leaving my husband to move to another country! What if you hated it there?' I asked. *Wait? Is that kind of what happened with Mark and me?*

'How can you know unless you try?' Quella seemed to have never looked back, and the more I got to know her, the more I realised she probably had no interest in kidnapping me at all. In fact, I must have felt comfortable in her company because I dozed off, and when I woke up, we were getting ready to land.

'Please fasten your seatbelts, we will be making our descent shortly,' the air hostess advised us through the speakers. The seatbelt sign turned on, and the echoing of all the passengers clicking their belts together rang throughout the plane. Quella was watching the end of a movie and sipping a Coke. She looked over at me.

'Sleep well?' she asked, taking an earphone out of one ear.

'When did I fall asleep? I still feel exhausted!' I told her, rubbing my face and looking out of the window. It was too dark to see anything.

'I'm not entirely sure. I must've bored you with one of my stories, because I looked over at one point and you were out,' she laughed. I groaned and leaned back on the window, hoping to get another quick nap in.

'Excited?' she asked me.

I nodded, keeping my eyes closed, my forehead cold from the icy window. 'I'm a bit nervous actually. I haven't travelled in a while!' I revealed, slowly opening my eyes.

'Oh, there is nothing to be nervous about! It's a touristy place, you'll be fine,' she assured me. When we finally landed, Quella and I stayed together until we picked up our luggage.

'MOMMY!' squealed a beautiful blonde-haired, pink-cheeked girl who was running our way. Quella's eyes lit up without even seeing who it was. She turned and crouched down as the little girl ran into her arms and hugged her tightly, picking her up from the ground.

'Darni, this is Mommy's new friend, Katelyn. Say hello.'

The little girl smiled but hid her face in the safety of Quella's neck.

'Oh, of course, now she wants to be shy!' Quella said sarcastically, poking Darni in the belly as she giggled hysterically.

'Welcome home, honey,' a burly bearded man said, kissing her on the cheek. He held his hand out to me, 'Rod.'

'Nice to meet you, I'm Katelyn. I had the pleasure of sitting next to Quella on the plane.' All of us laughed, mutually understanding it meant she talked my ear off.

'Did you hear that, Rod, *pleasure.*' She elbowed him cheekily. 'Can we drop her to her hotel, Green Palace?' Rod nodded and started wheeling a bag on each hand.

Once my phone had reception, I sent Adeline and Mom a quick text.

Landed in Reykjavík! I met a lovely tour guide on the plane named Quella and she's dropping me to the Green Palace Hotel. Speak soon. Love you!

I figured that text message would keep me somewhat safe, so I mentally compartmentalised any doubt and followed these three strangers, leaving the airport behind me.

19

Reykjavík

Rod brought the car around to us, and when we left the airport, I realised there was one thing I'd forgotten to do … check the weather for my arrival. I checked it during the planning but not before I actually left. It was snowing and colder than New York. We drove from Keflavík Airport toward Reykjavík, where I spent most of the car ride playing around with my camera and taking snaps of Quella and Rod talking to each other in Icelandic.

'How far is Reykjavík from the airport?' I asked, trying to include myself.

'Thirty miles; it takes some time,' Rod responded.

Gosh, that would have cost me a fortune for a taxi. Quella must have known.

'Wake up, sleepy, we've arrived!' Quella said, as Rod began taking my suitcase out. He didn't just take my suitcase out of the car, he walked it inside, leaving it by reception in the lobby. Quella stayed in the car but wound her window down to hand me her business card as I got out.

'Rest up, and tomorrow morning be ready at about nine. I still have some time off and would love to take you around the city.'

'Are you sure you? You just got home to your family,' I asked, already so grateful they had dropped me off at the hotel.

'I see them every day! I'll see you in the morning!'

'No, wait … here,' I pulled out American dollars and tried to hand it to her but she shooed it away before closing her window.

'You might want to get the right currency,' she yelled through the glass, laughing. Rod waved and got back in the car, and I watched as they slowly disappeared into the distance.

My stomach growled as I checked in, and my energy came back slightly after a shower. I added a couple more layers of clothing then headed back to the lobby to get dinner. The same blonde-haired Dutch woman that checked me in was standing by the reception desk by herself, doing something on the computer.

'Hi. I'm looking for something to eat, is there anything close by?' I asked her. She nodded, grabbed a nearby pamphlet, opening it up to show a map of the area.

'We are here,' she said with a strong accent, circling where the hotel was. 'Take your first left and third right,' she said as she drew a line on the map, 'this is where all the restaurants and cafes are located; you will find everything in this area.'

'Is there anything you recommend eating?' I asked.

'Something you must try here is our arctic char, cod and lamb … But any of these places will do a fine job. You will find all the produce here is fresh.'

'Perfect! Can I also change money here?' She turned behind her and pointed to their exchange rate. I had no idea if I was getting a good deal or not, but I wasn't sure if my credit card would work or what kind of fees it would charge me. I changed a couple of hundred dollars and walked out of the lobby feeling ravenous, and rich, with thousands of krónur.

It was dark and cold, and I was tired, grateful she marked the easiest way to get to food. For my own peace of mind, I double-checked street signs and made note of landmarks so I wouldn't get lost on the way back. Red mailbox. Bakery. Then I would know that the hotel was at the corner with a red mailbox and a bakery next door. There were plenty of people walking around, all seemingly tourists, and it wasn't long before I noticed restaurants and bars, but my indecisiveness had me walking the entire strip before giving up and pushing through the doors of a quaint little bar right at the end. I opened the stylish wooden doors and walked in slowly, cautiously. It was quite busy but relaxed. I walked past the coat rack, not trusting that it would be there when I left. *There are so many coats, how are people not leaving with the wrong one?* No-one was eating. *Do they serve food here?* I decided to have one drink, and if they didn't, I'd move on. A wave of anxiety rushed over me as I walked to the bar alone, it felt like everyone was watching me even though I didn't meet eyes with anyone. Sitting down on the bar stool, I looked around, not really knowing what to do with myself. I had never eaten or had a drink by myself in public before. I took my surroundings in, the wooden-framed pictures that were nailed on the walls and the dusty paintwork to give the impression this bar had been around for a long, long time. I ordered a house red and continued gazing; looking at the company I was surrounded with, so many faces I didn't recognise and many of them speaking languages I couldn't understand.

'Can I ask you a question?' I asked the bartender while he was pouring the wine.

'Of course you can, love,' he said with a thick Icelandic accent, 'you can ask me anything you want!'

'Do you serve food here, or can you recommend anywhere close by to eat? I'm starving!'

'We serve food here, but the kitchen is closed,' he said, with a little bit of excitement in his voice, 'we could probably do a plate for you if you don't mind sitting in the staff area?'

'Oh … really?' I hesitated, wondering once more if this was going to be the end of me. I looked around, hoping to see at least another plate.

I saw nothing.

'Des is right, the food here is the best,' the stranger sitting next to me said, winking. *I am starving.* I nodded.

'Oh, okay then. Well, give me your most popular meal then?' I said, mustering up as much enthusiasm as I could to hide the anxiety I felt inside. Des enthusiastically nodded.

'Grack! Icelandic specialty please!'

Grack? Who in God's name is Grack?

'Don't worry, Grack will sort you out!' Des said to me while pointing to my glass. 'Top-up?' I smiled and nodded again. He walked over and topped up my glass with wine and then took it to a little table in the corner, a bit of a nook that was hidden from the public. I followed him slowly, trying to figure out why he was doing a stranger a favour. Most places back home wouldn't open the kitchen if you were one minute past closing time, let alone completely cleaned and packed away.

I took my camera from my bag and started capturing things I liked about the bar, like the little nook where I was hidden. Sip of wine. *Click.* Sip of wine. *Click.* With every picture and generous gulp of the ruby red liquid courage I became more impressed with the bar and with myself. *I made it. I'm in another country by myself. I'm doing this.*

A tall, bearded man with a shaved head appeared from the kitchen, the apron around his waist telling me he must be Grack. He was holding a plate of beautifully prepared food with one hand, and the other rested on his lower back.

'Wow!' I said when he unveiled his creation. 'What do we have here?' I began taking pictures of it as he set it down in front of me.

'A platter of our arctic char, cod and lamb with potatoes,' he looked up at me with his bright blue eyes. I could tell he was pleased with himself.

'It looks amazing, thank you!' I said, placing my camera on the table, ready to unwrap the red napkin from the cutlery. I cut some of the char and tasted it, then some cod and then some lamb, savouring the flavours.

'Delicious!' I said through a mouthful of food. 'It melts in your mouth!' He put his hands together and bowed away graciously. 'I guess I did come to the right place!' I yelled to Des, in-between large mouthfuls. I finished my meal and another glass of wine before paying but Des refused to charge me for it. I was even more confused.

'The food is on the house,' he told me as I went to pay, 'we were experimenting with dishes for the new menu. It would have gone to waste otherwise, so thank you!' I wasn't sold on his response, but tipped to show I was grateful, and with a little sway in my walk, I made my way back to the hotel, the wine making my nose warm and cheeks red. It made the snow along the sidewalks prettier, the air feel cleaner and strangers look friendlier. It had been a long day, and I was ready for bed, and I knew nothing could wipe the smile from my face and the genuine content in my heart.

20

Magic

Ding ding ding ding! I woke up startled. Without moving my body, I darted my eyes around the room trying to recognise where I was. *I'm not at home.* No Luna next to me. It smelt different. My skin felt dry on the white linen. I wasn't sure if it was all a dream. *Am I really in Iceland?* I was sprawled across the queen-size bed and entwined in all the sheets, taking a few moments to find comfort in the sterile environment.

'Morning!' I said, surprised the receptionist was the same girl from the night before.

'Oh, good morning! Where did you end up eating last night?' she asked.

'I actually went to a little bar at the end of the street.' I explained through hand gestures where I turned. 'It was by accident. I was only going to have a drink before dinner, but the bartender recommended I eat there too. So, I did!'

'Which bar?'

'I can't remember the name. It had old pictures framed on the walls. It felt as if I'd gone back in time! Des and Grack?' The receptionist laughed. I could tell she wanted to say something.

'What?' I asked, confused by her reaction.

She hesitated. 'His name is Gottskalk.'

'Oh, you know them?' I asked.

'Des is my uncle, so I know Grack. It's a small place here.'

'I can see that,' I laughed, 'the food was amazing, please thank them again for me. I seemed to be the only one that was eating there, after they closed the kitchen. Is that usual around here?'

'I shouldn't really tell you this, but they haven't actually opened their kitchen yet … their grand opening is next month, so you must have been their guinea pig!'

'Well, that explains the free food!' I said, slightly annoyed they didn't tell me but amused all the same.

'Don't worry,' she said, possibly sensing my concern, 'Grack is an amazing chef and they're really working on bringing the essence of Iceland into their meals. They'll do well when they finally open, so count yourself lucky they picked you for taste testing.'

'I mean, I have nothing to compare it to, but it was good. So was the wine,' I responded honestly.

'I'll let them know,' she said, and then paused and looked at the time, 'you better hurry to breakfast so you don't miss it!'

It was 8:47am, which meant I had just over ten minutes to have breakfast before Quella arrived. I had a sneaky suspicion she was a punctual lady – being a tour guide, after all. I rushed to breakfast and grabbed a coffee, yoghurt and muffin and ate it while patiently waiting for Quella in the lobby.

9:01 … 9:06 … *Oh gosh. What if she isn't actually coming? Should I call her?* I decided to wait until 9:15am.

'Sorry I'm late, Kate!' Quella yelled as she rushed through the doors toward me, embracing me as if we were old friends.

'Oh, not a problem, thanks so much for doing this.'

'It's nothing really; I just had to battle Darni to get dressed for school. I think she wanted to spend the day with you too. You are a popular woman!' she laughed heartily. I didn't know if it was the sip of the hot coffee or being in her presence that gave me a rush of energy. She started walking back out the way she came, and I followed her outside. The sun was only just rising, and with the light snowfall, it was a beautiful sight.

'So, what's the plan?' I asked, excited for the day ahead as we got in the car.

'Have you eaten breakfast?' Quella asked.

'Well, I had something called skyr for breakfast,' I responded, and then held up my half-eaten muffin and nearly finished coffee. Quella laughed, possibly at my pronunciation of the word or possibly because I called yoghurt, muffin and a coffee breakfast.

We drove out of the city, passing by the different museums, churches and sculptures that Quella suggested I visit over the next few days that were walkable distance from the hotel. The further we drove out, the less there was around – the land mysteriously barren, yet eerily the most beautiful thing I had ever seen.

Having not travelled much, I didn't think the city of Rejkjavíc would be so built up and then be surrounded by nothing and everything. I assumed it would be quite a dreary place, where the skies were only varying shades of grey and nothing all that much to see besides the northern lights. There was nothing to take pictures of, yet it was also so picturesque. After about an hour, Quella handed me a paper bag with something buried inside, oil marks taking up most of the bag now. I peeked in to see a sugary pastry of some sort.

'It's called a kleina,' Quella said. 'It's an Icelandic pastry. Rod made it fresh this morning.' I opened the bag and started eating it, handing Quella a piece too.

'I don't remember how long you're here for?' she asked, a mouthful of the soft, buttery sort of doughnut. The thought of big, burly, manly Rod with an apron on in the kitchen amused me.

'Only five days, so three full days to see everything!' I said as I moved the food into my cheek to answer her, crumbs falling all over me.

'What else do you plan to do?' she asked.

'I'm not sure, I actually haven't sat down and decided on anything.' Now I was licking my fingers, trying not to miss any crumbs.

'You should go to the Blue Lagoon, it's a popular tourist attraction and so beautiful – expensive, but beautiful,' she responded, gesturing towards the direction of it with her left hand, her right one holding onto the wheel.

'Oh, thanks, I'll write that down!' I said excitedly, grabbing my phone and writing it in the notes app. I had never been to a geothermal spa before. I'd seen pictures of that huge outdoor spa in Hungary when I was planning my trip, where it looks freezing outside, yet everyone is in their bikini.

'We're here!' Quella said loudly. I rubbed my eyes and looked around to see where we were. There was a multitude of hills, and when I looked across the road, I could see steam coming from the ground, like little mini fires were surrounding us, except there was no fire. I put my camera around my neck and followed Quella as she started walking in the direction of a group of people in the distance. I was adjusting my camera when I heard a *PPSSHHHHHHHHH*. I looked up, startled, but couldn't see anything.

'You'll miss all the good stuff if you keep looking down at that camera,' Quella said cheekily, yet not slowing her pace. As I tried to keep up and take photos of the surreal steam surrounding us, I heard the *PSSSHH* again and a magnificent amount of water shot up from an unseeming hole in the ground and catapulted towards the sky. It came from nowhere and disappeared just as quickly.

'Whoa,' is all I managed to let out of my mouth.

'This is the Geysir geothermal area where the Strokkur geyser shoots water every six to ten minutes. Isn't it breathtaking? Think of the built-up power and force building beneath the surface. It all appears to be so calm

from our perspective, but imagine the energy brewing down there ...'
It was clear how fascinated Quella was, even after seeing it thousands of times I'm sure, but I could understand why. The best I could liken it to was a blowhole we had seen in Mexico, where it spurt out water, except this was a thousand times bigger and hotter. It felt like it had only been a second, but as I was more aware of what was happening this time, I could feel the pressure beneath our feet change ever so slightly and the earth sent small vibrations through our bodies. *PPSSSHHHHHHHH*. This time I was ready. *Click. Click. Click*. I adjusted my lens and kept going. *PPSSSHHHHHHHH. Click. Click. Click.*

I had taken so many pictures, hoping at least a couple captured the spectacular sight. We both stood there for a long while. What I liked about Quella was that we didn't always need to talk, we could enjoy each other's company without saying a word. It felt calm. It felt easy.

She didn't need to tell me that she was ready to leave either, we both just knew.

'Ten more minutes and we will be at the canyon of Hvita River,' she said. I was completely awake and full of curiosity during the next drive, taking photos of everything around me, from the flat land to the hills to the majestic waterfalls.

When we arrived at the canyon, she stopped the car and got out near a sign saying Gullfoss. I followed her lead. We walked and walked, and after some time, I could hear water. The sound of it felt closer with every step. Then I felt a sudden tremor and the unmistakable sound of thrashing water as waves came tumbling and crashing against each other. It got louder still, and before I knew it, we were face-to-face with a magnificent waterfall. Quella didn't need to tell me where we were; she didn't have to say anything. A sight like that needed no introduction. We stood, again mesmerised, and then walked in different directions, each toward whatever called us. I clicked away, wanting to remember this moment forever, cherish how unique it was. We spent a few minutes there, alone in our thoughts, before coming together again.

'Beautiful, huh?' she finally said, breaking our silence, already knowing my answer.

She's unbelievable!' I responded, neither of us taking our eyes off the falls.

We walked around, and I took a few more pictures, before making our way back to the car.

'You know what's crazy?' I asked. 'I came here for the northern lights, and to be honest, only that. I didn't know how much this place had to offer.'

'Yeah, it's magical here, no other place like it,' Quella agreed, nodding her head slowly, proud I felt the same way about her home.

We spent more time driving, stopping at another waterfall to eat lunch that Quella packed, and then we went to a glacier where movies had been filmed. All the while, Quella shared her knowledge about the sites, or stories from tours. A proposal here, a wedding there. We talked about where we wanted to travel to, we talked about work and our families, she even played me different Icelandic music. We talked about everything except Mark. No-one would have ever guessed Quella and I had only met the day before, a sheer coincidence of being seated next to each other on the plane. *How did I get so lucky?*

'I'll take you to my favourite place to eat for dinner,' Quella said as we started making our way back to the city, my stomach taking it as a cue to make noise. It was starting to get dark, and I had no idea where we were, or how long the drive back to the city was.

'That sounds perfect, and let me please pay for dinner, you have done so much for me today, it's the least I could do,' I said, letting her know her time wasn't lost on me. She seemed to not hear me – or she ignored me – and went on to tell me about the Thingvellir National Park and how the American and Eurasian tectonic plates were pulling apart at a rate of a few centimetres per year. I imagined a puzzle beneath the ground we were standing on that was moving with vibration, but then my mind trailed off, and I began thinking about Mark and what he was doing. *Would he have liked it here?*

21

Aurora Borealis

I was trying to push Mark out of my mind and remain present, focusing on what Quella was saying in case she quizzed me about it at dinner, but I couldn't.

'Still with me, Katelyn?' she asked, realising I must have been zoning out.

'Yeah, I'm sorry, this is absolutely amazing, but …'

'But what?' she asked me, turning the music down.

'My partner and I actually split up just before this trip …' I paused, 'and I keep thinking about him, maybe even wishing he was here with us.' I looked up, my eyes beginning to well, the burn in them I feel when I try and push the tears away.

'Oh, I'm so sorry to hear that. What happened?'

'After eight years, he told me he didn't want marriage and kids.' I wondered if Quella was going to bring up the fact I told her my husband was meeting me in Scotland. She didn't.

'From everything you've seen, would you have preferred to be back in New York with him?'

'No,' I responded, not knowing how honest the answer was.

'You know, the astronomer had a better relationship with the galaxy than he did with me,' Quella went on, 'Rod might not look like much, but he has a heart of gold and always puts our needs and wants over his own. He would do anything for me and Darni.' I barely knew Rod and Quella, but I could see it in the way he took our bags without hesitation and the way he listened so intently, dutifully, when Quella or Darni spoke to him.

'Mark is a good person too ...' I unnecessarily defended him.

'I'm sure he is; that's just my story, and that's all I'm sharing with you. I wasn't happy. I always tried to change the astronomer, but I've realised you can't change the other person; it really comes down to either accepting who that person is unconditionally or putting your needs first and making a change. I chose not to accept the way things were, so I made a change, and I left, and I made the move here and it's the best decision I've ever made.'

I liked that Quella wasn't telling me what to do, nor did she take my side for the sake of it. It wasn't advice, or an opinion, she was only sharing her story for me to draw from it whatever I needed to. *Would Mark change? Does he want to change? Do I want him to change?* I didn't have the answer.

'It's only your first day away from home, be gentle on yourself.'

I smiled at Quella and rested my head on the car window, straining my neck slightly but trying not to think about it. It made me feel like less weight was on my shoulders.

It was dark, and I could barely see any streetlights when we stopped suddenly. Quella got out of the car, and in panic, I followed what she was doing, not sure what I was looking for or what I needed to do. We were the only car around, our headlights beaming in front of us, showing us the long road ahead, snow pushed to the sides in high mounds.

'What's wrong?' I whispered even though no-one was around. I couldn't see anything, and it was freezing outside of the car. She didn't respond. 'Quel, what are you doing?' I asked louder, trying to tuck my face into my scarf. I turned to look at her and then followed her gaze straight up to the sky.

'Can you see it?' she asked, pointing toward the sky. I looked in the direction she was pointing but couldn't see a thing. I tried to focus my eyes, hoping they would adjust. *Is she pointing at a star?* I was starting to get agitated, and the second before I turned to leave and get back in the car, I saw it. I didn't know what I saw, maybe a glimmer? A sparkle? I started to see a very faint green glow toward the north of where we were standing; like the first moments of a sunrise. The green got brighter; it expanded across the sky, dancing before our very eyes. I couldn't say anything. I couldn't move. I was glued to the spot, in complete awe of what was in front of me. It'd been a dream of mine for years, but it was always just that ... a dream. I was living my dream.

'It gets me every time,' Quella said softly, in an almost hypnotic state.

'Crap!' I said, not wanting to miss this photo opportunity. I grabbed my camera from the passenger-side floor and started clicking away, adjusting the lens with every shot and trying to perfect my image. It had been a long time since I had taken photos in the dark, so I had no idea how good these were going to be.

'Enjoy it, Katelyn, it will always be in here,' Quella said smiling, tapping her forehead with her finger.

'Memories fade. I want to remember this forever,' I said, taking a quick snap of her tapping her head, 'but I guess I'll always remember that now too.' Quella laughed and shook her head. She gestured for me to give her my camera, and I watched as she changed settings on it. As she handed it back, the colours grew stronger. Oranges and reds made a brief appearance but didn't stay. The elegance of the lights dancing together was a sight to remember; I could have stood there for hours, never knowing what would happen next or how long it would stay, or when I would ever witness such a spectacle again.

When we finally decided to leave, we drove home in silence, watching all the different colours dancing above us. As we got closer to the city, they began fading. I didn't want to stop taking pictures though. I didn't want to forget any part of today.

'Last stop!' she promised, as she pulled the car up onto a driveway. I wasn't sure where we were until Darni ran out of the house and Rod appeared at the door.

'Your favourite place, huh?' I said cheekily, realising she had driven us to their home for dinner.

'You can't leave this place until you've tried Rod's cooking!' she stated matter-of-factly.

They had a modest home; one that looked lived in with things every-where – not just any things, but memorable things. There were trinkets on tables and shelves, there were carved animal statues and framed images of different destinations.

'What's that?' I asked, drawn to a wall of polaroids of different people in their living room. Some of them had postcards attached to them. I found more by the kitchen, with both Quella and Rod in adventurous locations around the world. I imagine these were taken before Darni was born, as they both looked a bit younger and skinnier, and Quella's hair was much longer.

'Oh, we used to put up couch surfers here, before Darni was born. We usually had Australians stay, but we'd get the odd traveller from the States or England.' I thought of Felicity. *I wonder where she is now?*

'Don't people get nervous about staying with strangers?' I asked, gen-uinely concerned.

Quella laughed her hearty laugh. 'Why? Are *you* nervous?'

I blushed. I didn't feel nervous at all, I felt like they were family.

Quella continued, 'Travellers are a special breed of people. We are wanderers, lovers, experience seekers, adventurers. We are birds of a feather that flock together. I mean, we have had a few super hippy odd-balls but never a truly bad experience. We stopped when I got pregnant, though. Actually, you're the first person we've had around like this for a very long time!'

The wall told so may stories, there were all sorts of people, and all of them sending letters and cards from wherever they were, thanking Rod and Quella for their hospitality.

'Speaking of which, you are more than welcome to stay here for the next few days if you like. I will be in and out with Darni, and Rod will mostly be at work.'

'Oh, that's so sweet, but I wouldn't want to impose like that.'

Quella pointed to her wall and frowned. 'I promise you, you won't be imposing, we would love to have you here.'

A part of me wanted to stay in my safe, quiet and clean hotel room to be alone for a little while, but the bigger part of me wanted to experience as much as possible.

'Well, okay then, but only if I get the couch so I can call myself a couch surfer?' I said, a big grin stretching out across my face.

'I'm glad you said that, otherwise I would have been sleeping on it,' Rod piped up from the kitchen. 'Quella still thinks we are twenty sometimes.' Quella rolled her eyes.

I put my backpack down and helped Rod set the table for dinner, drinking wine and listening to their adventures in bewilderment. We only noticed how late it was when I started yawning. Quella gave me a lift back to the hotel for my final night and we agreed that Rod would pick me up after work the next day, which gave me time to stroll around the city.

As I made my way back to my hotel room, thinking about everything Quella and Rod had done for me, I thought about how lucky I was to have met such kind people and witness such beautiful parts of this new country I was in. And for the first time, I realised how much of my own dreams I had pushed away for so many years. Then it hit me, it wasn't Mark who made me miss out … it was me.

22

Friends

It was still dark when I woke; knowing better than to look at the time, I lay there thinking about the night with Quella and Rod, and how crazy it was that they let complete strangers into their home – into their lives ... how easily they had made space for me. *I want to embrace all these new experiences ... but will I be safe?* I hadn't bought a local SIM card so was barely using my phone unless I had wi-fi, but as I lay there, I found Quella on social media, squinting at the glare of the screen that made my eyes slightly water. I followed her and scrolled through her page – it was her to a T. I also checked Adeline's and Eva's, my Mom's and my siblings. I found myself checking Mark's – still no updates.

Almost as if the universe was trying to tell me something, my phone made a soft *beep*, letting me know I received an email, the name making my skin tingle.

Dear Katie,

I want you to know that I did think about seeing you off at the airport, I just didn't know how you would have felt about it. I should have said bye, I'm sorry. I hope you're having a good time and it's everything you imagined it would be. It would mean a lot to me if we could speak while you are away ... if you'd like to. I'm not sure what the time difference is ... In fact, I'm not even sure where you are right now … I'll leave the ball in your court.

Mark.

The email caught me by surprise. Even though I'd thought about Mark, I didn't expect him to make contact. *Do I respond now? Should I respond now?* I decided not to. Not yet. I didn't even know what to say, or where to begin, or how I felt. I put my phone back on the bedside table and got out of bed, trying to process what I had read. I packed my suitcase, battling my mind not to think about it.

I was in such a daze as I went to check out, I nearly walked into two girls chatting away in the lobby. They had a bag with bathers and a towel.

'Oh! Are you going to the spa today, by any chance?' I asked as I handed the receptionist my room key, surprised I had asked strangers like that.

'We are!' one of the girls said delightfully. She leaned forward as she responded, blatantly ending the conversation with her friend. 'Are you?'

'Yes, I really wanted to, but I had to check out. Mind if I join you? I can pull it all out of my suitcase quite easily now.'

'Not at all, we're just waiting for the bus. It's getting here soon.' The girl who responded reminded me of an old school friend. She had bright green eyes and a sweet dimple on her left cheek. Her friend was a little quieter, and her body language was difficult to read. Probably how I looked when Quella first met me.

'Thanks, I wasn't sure how to get there, to be honest. I would have spent a fortune on an Uber.'

'Oh, don't worry, we had to ask the desk. We decided to pick beer over the taxi!' The green-eyed girl handed me a beer. 'Janine,' she said.

'Hi Janine, I'm Katelyn.' I took the beer from her hand and placed it on the floor next to my now-open suitcase while I tried to pull the towel from the corner I stuffed it in. Once I had everything I needed shoved into my backpack, I looked over at her friend and held out my hand, 'Really lovely to meet you too!'

'Emily.' She shook my hand politely in response. Emily had shoulder-length straight brown hair, freckles over her entire face and omitted an innocence about her.

'Are you travelling alone, Katelyn?' Emily asked.

'I am. It was a last-minute spontaneous adventure. I quit my job and broke up with my boyfriend,' I paused, 'essentially, I'm having a midlife crisis.'

They both laughed, and I knew we were going to get along just fine. Janine was the first to crack the beer, and I followed suit, forcing the yeast-tasting cheap poison into my body at 10:05am, wondering how I did it in my twenties.

'You're a free woman,' said Janine, holding her beer up to cheers me.

'I am!' I said as the bus pulled up at the perfect moment, letting me get away with not having another sip and strategically leaving it on the receptionist's desk.

'Have you seen the northern lights?' I asked, continuing the conversation on the bus. Janine and Emily sat down beside each other, and I sat at the seat in front of them, awkwardly twisting my body around to face them.

'No, we went on a tour and stayed until about 11pm but then gave up. They said it was an 83% likelihood, but anyway, it wasn't our night.'

'I guess you can't predict Mother Nature,' I said cheekily, repeating what Quella had said to me.

'Where are you from, Katelyn?' Janine asked.

'I'm from New York. How about you?'

'We're from Sydney, we're backpacking around Europe at the moment!'

'I hear a lot of Australians do that, I don't know how you all get the time and the money!'

'We train our kangaroos pretty well, actually,' Janine joked.

'Where are you off to next?' I asked.

'London!' they said excitedly at the same time.

'Ohh, nice. I'm meeting family in Scotland soon, I should really stop over while I'm so close.'

'Well, our flight is the day after tomorrow, you're more than welcome to join us if you like? We don't really have a plan. We are going with the flow.'

Another kind offering? I thought about what Quella said, about the kindness of travellers. I spoke with Janine and Emily the entire way there. We couldn't believe our eyes when we finally got to the Blue Lagoon. It was in the middle of nowhere and surrounded by volcanic rock. There were strict instructions on showering, drinking, eating and even paying for everything with the bracelets we were given. We walked outside in our bikinis, the four-degree air biting our skin, but the warm, turquoise water calling us in. It was beautiful, the white steam effortlessly dancing above the water.

'AAAAAYYYYYY!' I heard coming from the other side of the lagoon. Janine and Emily gestured for me to follow them, snapping me back to reality.

'We met a few other backpackers at the hotel a couple nights ago and we all agreed to meet here today,' Janine explained. 'We weren't sure if anyone else would turn up, but we wanted to come anyway.'

I flowed like the water, smiling and saying hello to anyone Janine and Emily introduced me to. More strangers, yet they all instantly felt like friends. It was like I had known them for such a long time. *How is it possible that for the eight years I lived in Manhattan, I haven't met a single friend, but halfway across the world, I have met someone new around each corner?* I watched as these friends came and went, but no-one seemed to mind. There didn't seem to be any restrictions or expectations, just friendship. Everyone seemed to have a knack for talking to whoever stood next to them, even if it was a family, an elderly couple or kids. *Is it because everyone is on holiday? Is it a certain kind of earthly dust that sits on the skin of travellers?* I took this opportunity to venture around the lagoon by myself, needing some quiet time to recharge. The entire lagoon was shallow enough to walk so I did a lap, wishing I had my camera with me. It was only as the temperature started dropping that more and more people started to leave; it was getting darker, and the wrinkles on my fingertips and toes told me it was time to go.

'What's tonight's plan?' I heard one of the guys ask as I walked back to Janine and Emily.

'You tell us,' they answered him, their faces covered with a clay mask.

'Shall we all go back to that bar tonight? The beers were cheap, and it was good the other night.' Everyone seemed to agree.

'Are you coming, Katelyn?' Janine asked.

'Yeah, why not!' I wasn't sure if Quella and Rod would mind, but I figured they wouldn't. 'I'm staying with some friends in town though; they are picking me up from the hotel at five. I will have dinner with them and then catch an Uber to wherever you guys are?' I said, the girls nodding, as we got out of the water and went back to the locker rooms.

We exchanged phone numbers, social media pages and a hug, before they headed back to the hotel, leaving me once more to soak up some alone time. I took my time showering and even managed to slip in for a very expensive one-hour back massage. While I waited for Rod, I walked to the outdoor area and took some photos, mesmerised by the colours, the travellers enjoying themselves and completely forgetting there was an email that I needed to respond to.

23

Notes

I woke up to the sound of Quella making coffee in the kitchen; she must have seen me cover my head with the blankets.

'Would you like me to make you one, little miss 4am?'

'No, thank you,' my husky voice barely managing to respond. I rolled into the couch so I could bury my head into it. I heard her chuckle. 'Did I make any noise when I got in?'

'I don't think you did anything, I think you literally opened the door and face-planted the couch. I heard nothing except the door open and close.'

'I feel awful,' I groaned, voice muffled by the couch.

'Good night, then?' Quella asked, putting a bottle of water on the coffee table. 'It's still early. Drink water and rest up, maybe you'll be able to do something this afternoon?'

'I hope so. I don't want to waste a day.' I could hear that Quella was close by, so I rubbed my face and sat up, not wanting to be rude. I sighted the water. As I reached to get it, I could see make-up on my hand – my mascara was smudged, and I could only imagine what my hair was doing. I laughed. *What a mess I am.* I felt that first sip of water hydrate my entire body, the coolness on my tongue travel through my chest and to my stomach. It felt so good. I drank the entire bottle in the same time it took Quella to take two sips of her coffee. I told her all about the night and then she slipped off to work. It was only once everyone left the house that I looked at my phone for the first time, nervous at what messages or photos I might find in there.

The first thing I noticed was a message from Janine.

Hi Katelyn, a few of us are heading to one of the volcanoes today. Emily is bailing after last night. Would you like to buy her ticket?

I looked at the time. It was 8:50am.

What time? I replied.

A little after 10:00am.

Oh god. That's so soon. Okay, I'll be at your hotel for then! I jumped up and got ready, my mouth dry and my skin excreting that pungent odour of toxins from a big night out. I didn't think just one shower was going to get rid of it.

When I got to the hotel, everyone was waiting outside for the shuttle. The first person I saw was Janine running over to the Uber, looking the opposite to how I felt.

'How do you have so much energy?' I asked her, not even able to force a smile, let alone a run. She laughed, thinking I was joking. She must be younger than me.

'My tummy isn't right after those late-night hot dogs, though,' she said, rubbing her belly.

'Ohh, I forgot about those! Maybe that's why I'm not feeling too flash either!'

'Or it was the tequila?' I shuddered just hearing her say the word.

We watched as the bus pulled up and we all piled in; the tour guide introduced himself and gave us some Reykjavík history. He asked where we were all from, and if we were having a good time and said how the hike wasn't too difficult. *Hike? What hike?* My tummy rumbled.

'There's a hike?' I turned and asked Janine.

'Well, we have to walk up the volcano, so maybe that's what he's talking about?'

'Up the volcano?' I asked her. I didn't know if my body would be able to get through the day with the state I was in and tapped out of most of the conversation so I could nap, consciously telling my body to prepare itself.

As we drew nearer and nearer to the car park, the volcano we were to hike up looked bigger and bigger. I had no idea how I was going to make it to the other side, let alone back, but before I knew it, we were on the way.

'You know I've never hiked up anything before, right?' I said to Janine, but she wasn't listening.

We started walking from the car park; the rocky terrain was wet from the melted snow. The landscape was all browns and greys and olive greens, and the clouds were making it difficult to see. We all walked on the pathway at a slow pace, and the guide said it would only take about an hour, which gave me a bit of relief.

Sometimes we walked in conversations, sometimes we walked in silence, admiring the eery surroundings or concentrating on our step as the pathway lessened and the steep parts needed our focus. It got colder and windier as we got higher, and despite the sweat at the base of my lay-ers, my toes started to get cold, and I realised my single pair of socks and sneakers were not the most appropriate footwear. I heard someone say 'wow' and I instinctively looked up, seeing bright orange lava popping out of the main peak.

'Whoa,' I said, stopping, 'an actual erupting volcano. That's crazy, isn't it?' Even I was confused and not fully comprehending how unusual the sight was. I couldn't believe I was looking at lava, an actual active volcano. I saw Janine take out her SLR camera from her backpack and adjust the lens to take a few photos, and then realised I had forgotten mine in the rush and the hangover.

'That's a gorgeous camera,' I said, admiring it.

'Thanks, it's a bit dated now, but I love it.'

'I don't think it matters how old it is, as long as it does the job how you want it to,' I said. 'I stopped taking photos of things years ago, but my parents bought me a new one before I left, kind of like a break-up present, but I forgot it. I barely know how to use it!'

'Maybe when we can get back, I can show you? I use heaps of different ones in class so might be able to show you a couple tricks.'

'That would be so nice. Any tips on how to use my phone for now?' I held my phone between my thumb and pointer finger, wobbling it.

'I do, actually.' She took my phone and pressed a few buttons, taking pictures and then showing me again. I nodded excitedly, seeing the differences in each that she showed, and then we both clicked away. It was an incredible sight to see, and I was saddened when it was time to have a quick snack and then turn around to head back to the bus. I held Janine's water while she put her camera into the backpack and pulled out some snacks.

'What's that?'

'It's my journal. I just add little things everywhere I go – nothing that exciting.' The journal was falling apart, but there was no doubt it was riddled with stories and memories, which added to the beauty of it. She saw my curiousness and pulled it out and handed it to me. I flipped through, admiring all her little souvenirs.

I gasped, looking at a little paper. I didn't say anything, I held up the page to her and pointed at it.

'Oh, I met this backpacker a few months ago in Rome, and she gave it to me.' Janine smiled fondly at the note, it read:

Happiness is not something you postpone for the future; it's something
you design for the present – Jim Rohn

'I was going through a pretty tough time, and I met her at a hostel in a female-only dorm. We really connected and she gave me some good advice. She was gone the next day but left this for me on top of a packet of Tim Tams.'

'What's a Tim Tam?'

'Only the best chocolate biscuit you will ever eat in your life,' Janine responded, looking very confident with her statement.

'Well … let me show you something.' I reached into my purse that was in my backpack and showed her the one Felicity had dropped into my pocket the time I saw her in Brooklyn.

'No way!' Janine yelled, comparing the FH at the bottom of both the notes.

'It's funny, I kind of told her my problems when I bumped into her in Brooklyn … she must have slipped it into my pocket without me knowing. She was definitely part of the reason I finally found the confidence to go on this trip.' It felt serendipitous.

We both sat there, eating snacks, staring at an active volcano, feeling nostalgic. When we got back to the hotel, one of the guys handed everyone a beer. As he handed me one, I instinctively took a step back.

'No thanks, I only just survived the hike today, I can't do this to my body again.' I laughed, a small bit of vomit rising in the back of my throat and then going back down again.

'The only way to feel better is to have another,' he said, opening it for me and pushing it into my hand, winking. I laughed and had a sip, then handed my beer to Janine.

'Ohh, I forgot! What time are you and Emily leaving tomorrow?' I asked, forgetting I needed to tell her I wanted to come.

'Not until the evening, so another big night is on the cards,' she laughed.

'Think I should change my flight?' I needed her to say yes.

'You should!' she said, unlocking her phone and looking for flights.

'I mean, how much longer could you really be here for? I'm pretty sure you've seen everything … AND I can teach you all about photography when we get to London!'

'How much would it be?'

'It's only a three-hour flight, so like, maybe seventy dollars?'

'No way, are you serious?'

'Yup!' She held her phone in front of me to show a seat left on her same flight. 'Coincidence? I think NOT!'

'I mean, okay, why not!' I said after only a moment's hesitation. *What have I got to lose?* And just like that, I went online and changed my ticket from Iceland to London.

24

Goodbye

The only sad thing about my out-of-character spontaneous decision to go to London was having to say goodbye to Quella, Rod and Darni. We'd only known each other a short while, but they felt like family now. I missed going out again so I could spend my last night in Iceland with them.

'It's been so lovely having you!' Quella said at the dinner table, a hint of sadness in her smile. Darni gave me a hug before Rod picked her up to put her to bed.

'Are you heading out tonight?' Quella asked.

'No, I really wanted to hang out with you guys!' I said, topping both our glasses up with wine.

'Rod can take you to the airport tomorrow,' she stated, not even knowing what time my flight was.

'Thank you, both. Really, I mean it. You've been so supportive and generous with everything, and it means so much to me. Please let me know when you're in New York; I'd love to return the favour!'

'If you're even there!' she responded, raising her eyebrows with a cheeky smile. She didn't think I would go back to New York. *New York. Oh, crap! Mark!* My eyes widened quickly, realising I hadn't told her yet.

'Quella! Mark emailed me!' She shook her head and scrunched her nose in a disapproving gesture. 'I haven't responded, I don't know what to do. He said he wanted to stay in touch. Should I?'

'Do you miss him?' she asked, taking a sip from her glass.

'I do, I think about him all the time … but I wouldn't take back anything. It pushed me to go on this trip and … and I don't think I could be any happier than I am right now. Is that bad?'

'No, that's not bad. It's the truth,' she said. I knew she understood how I was feeling.

Maybe that's a sign,' I responded, 'but I don't want to regret it at the same time. What if our life is us being together, but I always travel alone?'

'Respond to his email; maybe see where it leads? There is no harm in it,' she said. I nodded. I held up a glass and made a toast to her and Rod, just as he re-entered the room.

'To family in all the right places,' I said, the muscles in my cheeks aching from all the laughing and smiling.

'To family in all the right places!' they repeated. Rod didn't stay up too much longer, but Quella and I did. She felt like an old friend – one of those friends you can talk to for hours and hours and there was still so much to say.

'Oh wow! It's 1:50am. You've got work tomorrow!'

'And you've got a flight to catch!' She took the last sip of wine and stood up from the couch, placed the empty wine glass by the kitchen sink and walked over to me.

'It's been a pleasure, Katelyn, truly. We'll all miss you and your kind spirit. It's been really beautiful watching you come out of your shell. But we'll see you in New York, I know it.' We hugged, a tear forming in my eye and then dropping heavily onto Quella's shirt.

'I'll send you a picture and a postcard,' I said as I pointed to her couch surfing wall, 'and when I'm back to visit, you better have it on there!'

'It'll take pride of place, don't you worry!' And with that, Quella went to bed, leaving me alone in the lounge room, finishing my last sip of wine. I opened my email and began drafting my response to Mark.

Hi Mark,

I understand why you weren't there; please don't worry.

I'm really well, thanks. This trip has been more than I could have ever imagined. I'm currently in the capital of Iceland, Reykjavík, and am off to London tomorrow with a couple of Australian girls I have met.

I hope you are well also, give a few kisses to Luna for me if you see her. Am sure Mom is spoiling her.

Katelyn.

I didn't know if I wanted to give him a reason to reply, so I didn't ask any questions. *Maybe it will fizz after this? Do I want it to fizz?* The email was to let him know I was okay, and that there were no hard feelings. It felt good to press send, and that's how I knew I had done the right thing.

25

Sown

Before I knew it, I was on the plane with Janine and Emily, London bound. I didn't get to sit next to them because I'd only booked my flight the night before. Instead, I was sitting next a stout man with thick-rimmed glasses and a tweed suit. *How very British.* He looked like he belonged in first class, not economy. I smiled at him as I settled in, taking my camera out before kicking my backpack under the seat in front of me.

'Photographer?' he asked, looking away from his phone for a moment.

'Oh, no, I wish … It's more of a hobby, really,' I said shyly.

'If it's a hobby, it's a passion. If it's a passion, don't be afraid to put a label on it,' he said, pausing before adding, 'if you wanted to, anyway. Can I take a look?' I was taken aback, I hadn't really shown anyone my photos before.

'I guess. I haven't used a camera like this in years. My parents gave it to me before I left.' I wasn't quite sure why I was defending myself. I watched him as he flicked through all the images. He had a stern, unfaltering expression on his face, one where I couldn't figure out what he was thinking.

'You said you used to use cameras like this? Why did you stop?' he asked, not looking at me.

'Well … I don't really know. I thought about it, but I guess I didn't think I was good enough to make a career out of it, maybe? Not enough money in the arts and all.' I stopped there, not knowing what else to say.

'Why did you think that?' he pressed on.

'The advice I got, I guess. I ended up studying finance … I knew that was stable …' my response laced with pauses. He made me feel uneasy, like I had to justify my decisions.

'And so you went into finance?'

'I did,' I hoped I sounded convincing.

'And so, was that the career for you, then?' he continued.

I sat quietly. *Is it?* I didn't think it was. He looked up at me when he realised I didn't want to respond. 'These are really good!'

'What are?' I was confused.

'Your pictures, of course,' he said, 'the composition and the colours and the angles – wow.'

'Oh. I was just playing around,' I shrugged, embarrassed; aware my face was likely going pink with the compliment.

'I guess that's the beauty of it. It's like you are seeing something different for the first time.' I like that he said that. I did feel like my pictures allowed me to see so much more when I looked back at them and that's why I loved taking them. 'Have you thought about selling any of your work?' I snorted, assuming he was joking. He stared at me.

'Oh, you're serious?' I said after a moment. He started to look agitated.

'You should take pride in your work, there is a future in this for you if you want it.' He reached inside his tweed jacket and handed me a business card.

'My name's Christian. I'm an art distributor working primarily out of London. You have a great eye and I'd love to share your vision with others. I want you to email me if you're interested in selling any of your prints.' I took his card, wondering if there was some kind of ulterior motive.

'Really?' I asked him, not believing that it was possible for someone to willingly pay money for what I'd taken.

'I'm serious. And those photos? Of the restaurant? You could probably reach out to the owner and see if he is interested in buying the ones of the space and food.'

'I will. Thank you.' I put his card in my purse; still unsure whether to take it seriously or to simply forget the whole thing had happened. He handed my camera back and got back on his phone. *Would Des and Grack really want those photos?* I sat there for a moment thinking about how crazy it was to meet another traveller and hop on a last-minute flight to London with them, to then be seated next to an art distributor who claimed to like my work? *And ... did I just call my pictures work? Could I truly be paid for this?* I began looking at my images again, in greater detail. Such beautiful memories. *I guess they are pretty good.*

26

London

We didn't check into our hostel until late, but Emily and I already knew the first question Janine was going to ask when we got there.

'Pub crawl?' I looked at Emily and laughed. Emily nodded and grabbed her purse.

'You guys go; I'm going to hang back.'

'Aww, c'mon, we just got to London!' she said excitedly.

'I know. Next time,' I said, urging them out of the room. They hesitated, but knew I needed some time to myself. Once they left, I took a breath and looked around. It was the first time I had stayed in a hostel and was grateful they picked the female-only four-bed dorm with a private ensuite instead of the eighteen-person mixed dorm. It didn't look like anyone else had checked in yet as the last bed was bare. The room was up three sets of stairs; I never understood why such buildings had no lift. The walls were painted beige – scuff marks and paint chips everywhere – a set of steel lockers and a small white fan in the corner. The window overlooked a busy street with dated curtains opened to let fresh air into the room. I threw the sheets onto one of the top bunks as the thought of anyone seeing my face sleeping creeped me out. I knew it was worth the experience, but it was still slightly overwhelming as I climbed up the creaking ladder and put the sheets on the old mattress, wondering what stories this mattress, or these sheets, could tell me.

When my bed was made and I felt I had some kind of order, I headed back down the three flights of stairs and out the door, taking in the fresh, cool air. I quickly checked the maps app on my phone, downloaded a ten-kilometre radius and then set off in no particular direction with one goal in mind: to wander, to wonder.

For years I had dreamt of wandering around this thriving city, in silence, by myself. The air felt full of activity and the streets were busy as I caught eye of London Bridge and made my way there. It wasn't as cold as Iceland, but I still had to wear my coat and boots. It was easy to identify the locals from the tourists. The locals were rushing around with their heads down, whereas the tourists stopped to observe the towering buildings and stare in awe at street performers. London was pure chaos, a different type to New York, but it was beautiful.

I made my way to Leicester Square and sat on a bench eating an M&S grab-and-go salad, people-watching. A tall, attractive man, with dark features and a dimple on his right cheek caught my eye and I froze, he looked strangely like Mark. He looked at me and smiled, but kept walking with a fast pace – surely a local. I wondered what Mark was doing and whether he was going to reply to my email or not. *If he was with me, would we be people-watching together, or would we be in some fancy hotel ordering room service?* I knew I would never have experienced a hostel dorm room if he were here. My mind wandered to Christian and whether people would really buy my pictures. *Would selling my images take the love I have away from it? Could I move away from my home for the sake of following my passion? Could I live here, in this very city? Is it too busy? Would I feel safe? Could I live so far away from my family?* It was hard enough leaving Quella and not knowing when I would see her again. *Could I truly live a life abroad? … Family – I better email Alice.* I sent her a quick email as I roamed the cobbled streets.

Hi Alice,

Letting you know I arrived in London this evening.

I will stay here a week or so before heading to Edinburgh.

Will make sure to update you on my travel plans once I've landed. Hope

you're well – I'm excited to meet you in person!

Katie x

I continued to entertain the idea of becoming a photographer and not going back to New York. *Maybe this is the reason I came here in the first place? Maybe meeting Christian was pure fate?* But I'd never really believed in the concept of fate before. I've always felt that life just *is*. I believed the rich and famous were somehow the lucky ones.

That night, I dreamt I didn't live in New York anymore. My dream wasn't in this city though – it was near water, and it wasn't the Thames. I could see a sunny blue sky through the glass windows. The art studio wasn't mine. It did, however, have a small area featuring my work. It was a peaceful dream, as if it was some kind of external reassurance telling me I was going to be alright.

The dream was disturbed at roughly 4am, when the footsteps of what I thought was three drunk girls stumbled through the door 'trying' to be quiet. I first heard the door, and then talking, or what they would have thought was whispering, and then the rustling of bags.

'Janine? Emily?' I whispered.

'Yeaahhhhhh,' they both said in perfect unison, prompting a fit of muffled giggles.

'Walking tour tomorrow morning at 10:30am? It's free.'

'Okay, Katie-Patie,' Emily responded. I wasn't sure who the other girl was. *Maybe they knew the girl that was sleeping on the last bunk bed?* The soft rustling continued for a few moments before it went quiet. I drifted back off to sleep, hearing the ocean in my dreams.

27

Confusion

The girls didn't wake up of their own accord in the morning; they woke up because they heard me getting ready. Unlike them a few hours earlier, I wasn't trying to be quiet.

'What time is it?' Emily asked through a loud yawn, stretching both arms up above her head, toes pointing straight forward.

'It's 10am, you have half an hour.' Emily didn't open her eyes or acknowledge my answer, but Janine groaned.

'Impossible,' she said. I snorted unintentionally; secretly smug that I wasn't feeling how they looked.

'You guys don't have to come,' I said.

'I'm up, I'm up,' Janine responded, rolling back the duvet and making her way towards the bathroom. I knew she would look perfect in about ten minutes.

'I guess I am too,' Emily said, still lying in bed with her eyes closed.

'How was your night?' I noticed there wasn't a third girl in the room.

'Janine made out with some English girl,' Emily giggled.

'Ohh, I knew I heard three of you last night,' I said, laughing, 'she left so quickly?'

'Thank god, we didn't even do anything when we got back. I think we both passed out. It was so uncomfortable trying to share a single bed,' Janine walked back into the room from the ensuite like she was brand new.

'Sooooo … a good night?' I said, laughing at their antics, wondering if I would have joined in if I was in my twenties too.

'I'll wait for you both at reception. I'm leaving in ten, okay?' I left the room so they could focus on getting ready, killing time by scrolling through social media. Felicity was in Florida. Mom posted a picture of Luna. Then I noticed an email from Mark.

Dear Kate,

I'm so glad you responded and really happy to hear you've had a good trip so far. I'd be lying if I said I didn't miss you. A part of me regrets not coming with you. Where will you be for your birthday? How would you feel about me visiting you for a few days?

Mark x

I gulped. *Mark? Coming here for my birthday?* I couldn't believe it was something he'd do. Not that he'd actually done it yet. I started typing a response as Janine and Emily came running down the stairs.

'Are we late?' they said, flustered.

'No, no, it's fine. Let's go.' I said bluntly, allowing it to save in my drafts for later.

'Are you okay?' Janine asked as she hurriedly tied her golden hair into a bun.

'Yeah, I'm fine,' I responded, not wanting to get into it. We made our way to the walking tour, which started at Covent Garden.

'How did you hear about the tour?' Emily asked.

'I was googling things to do last night, and it came up on Tripadvisor.'

'That's cool, I didn't know there were free tours.'

'We have to tip at the end, but it's whatever you think it's worth and so much cheaper than the cost of an actual tour.' I said, acting as if it wasn't the first time I had been on one.

We joined the group as the tour guide was introducing himself. I didn't hear too much, only that his name was Toby and he was from Germany. He was dressed well, his head covered by a black beanie. He led us through the city of London, explaining the history of the Tower Bridge, Tower of London, St Paul's Cathedral and Shakespeare's Globe theatre, Janine showing me tips and tricks with my camera as we went. There was much to take in, and after about thirty minutes I zoned out and soaked up the winding streets and grand architecture of the place.

'Can we go get some food now?' Janine moaned, not paying attention either, as the group kept on walking on. I didn't want to leave, but I could tell the girls were getting antsy.

'Just wait until I can give the tour guide some money,' I said, scoping out an opportunity.

'Who cares, let's just go. Those other people did,' she said.

'I'm not going to do a runner, guys, we can give him some cash!' Janine looked embarrassed and handed me a five-pound note; Emily followed suit. I made eye contact with the tour guide and waved him over.

'I'm really sorry, we have to leave, but thanks so much!' I handed him fifteen pounds, and took both of his hands to shake one of mine.

'Thank you, most people don't do that!' he responded graciously. The girls waved at Toby, thanking him as well, before the group walked in the opposite direction.

'So, ladies, where would you like to go?' I asked.

'Fancy Camden Town?' Emily suggested. I'd read about this place, full of markets and food stalls. Without another word, we all turned and made our way to the nearest tube station.

'We definitely don't have one of these in Sydney,' Janine said.

'Where is Camden Town?' I asked, looking at the maze trying to figure it out.

'There. But I have no idea how we get there,' she said, pointing to the stop.

'Oh, that's easy, we have to take this line to there, and then switch the tube here and here,' I said, mapping out the direction with my hand. Both girls stared at me blankly, so I took charge and led the way.

'JERK CHICKEN!' Janine yelled as soon as we exited the tube station. She ran off, and Emily and I hurried after her in an attempt to stay close in the busy streets.

'We don't get much of this in Australia, it's been my absolute fave since we discovered it,' she said, as I watched them pull apart the meat and mix it with the rice and beans. The smells wafting through the area were mouth-watering, a multitude of different cuisine and cultures.

'Have you been okay today, Katelyn?' Emily asked as she wiped her mouth with the napkin. 'You seem a bit down?' I didn't want to lower the mood, but I did need to talk to someone about it. About him.

'I need a drink,' I said, as I pointed to a comedy bar that was overlooking the canal. Janine and Emily were always down for a drink, and it was over a G & T that I told them what had been going on with Mark.

'Oh wow, do you miss him?' Janine asked, making sense of the break-up comment I made hiking up the volcano.

'I do. Mostly when I'm reminded of him in some way. His favourite food, or someone with the same features as him. Sometimes it's because I'm alone and I see couples. But I don't know if I miss him for the right reasons.'

'I mean, if you can't stop thinking about him,' Emily said, 'maybe it would be nice for him to meet you for your birthday? It will show him trying for you and your relationship.'

'I guess the real question would be, if you said no and ended it forever, and both moved on with your lives, would you one day regret it?' Janine added as she took the last sip of her beer. I didn't respond, but I knew the answer. I would wonder. I sat there with my new friends, putting together an email to Mark.

Hi Mark,

I'll be honest; at first, I wasn't sure how to respond to this. I've been trying to travel with you for such a long time, so I know I shouldn't say no if you're feeling ready for it … Maybe it would be good. I'm leaving for Edinburgh next Thursday and will ask Alice if it's okay for you to stay.

Will be in touch soon.

Katie x

I looked at the 'x', the little kiss. I thought I'd leave a small romantic gesture to end the email. I still couldn't quite believe that he'd come all the way to Scotland for my birthday. *Could we even travel together in this new way that I've discovered?* I wasn't sure about the answer, but I did miss him, and I did want to see him again. It had been so long since I'd seen a familiar face; someone that I didn't have to repeat my life story to. There and then, I booked a sleeper train the following Thursday from London to Edinburgh and then forwarded the email receipt to Alice with an additional note:

Hi Alice,

I've booked the Caledonian Sleeper from London to Edinburgh next Thursday. Let me know your address and I'll book an Uber once I arrive.

Cannot wait to see you!

Love Katie x

The decision settled my racing mind and nervous heart. I joined back into the conversation with Janine and Emily, talking about what else we were going to do while we were there. We got on our phones and booked tours, and wrote down places we wanted to visit like the Buckingham Palace, and while a part of me wondered if I could keep up with these young twenty-year-old Australians, I knew our time would soon be over and it would slow back down once I was with my family. I was so excited to meet Alice and Uncle Pat, someone that was so dear to my mom.

For now, though, it was time to relax and enjoy all that London had to offer.

28

Family

I stood at the Edinburgh train station by myself, trying to figure out the best place for the Uber pick-up. Alice and I never found a moment to chat, but she'd emailed me their address. As I moved my way through the crowd, I noticed a familiar face and a sign with my name.

WELCOME, KATELYN! It was Alice holding the sign. I recognised her face from her social media. I naturally put my bags down as soon as I got to her and hugged her tightly. She felt as friendly as she looked.

'You didn't!' I said to her, referring to the fact she picked me up.

'Of course I was going to pick you up,' she said. I could feel her warm ear press against my cheek, her hug as tight as mine. Alice had an energy about her, although her social media made her seem quieter than she was, I instantly felt at ease in her company.

'Come along now,' she said with her thick Scottish accent. She picked up my bags before I had a chance to lift them myself and led me to her car in the car park. It was raining, the clouds grey and the air moist.

'It's always miserable this time of year,' Alice laughed apologetically. 'Well, actually, it's like this all year round but you have come at the peak worst time!'

'This isn't too bad, we can get some pretty harsh winters in NYC, the blizzards are horrendous sometimes,' I said. I could see some of my sister in Alice's face, as I subtly scanned it from the passenger seat.

'How was the train? I want to hear all about Iceland! I'd love to see it one day! You're so lucky!' she said excitedly. Though I appreciated her words, I didn't like hearing I was 'lucky'. It made me feel like I hadn't given anything up, or that all of this had come easily. It hadn't. I had quit my job, left Mark and was so confused about my future. I let it go though, knowing her intention wasn't to make me feel that way.

'Iceland is a mystical place, and the northern lights took my breath away. I didn't realise how much there was to see there. I cut my trip short so I could go to London with the Aussie girls I met,' I said, thinking about the beautiful landscapes, and of course, Quella. I could have gone on and on about my travels, but I hadn't mastered the fine line between storytelling and what some people might hear as gloating. Alice continued to ask questions and I gave her all the answers, asking her questions in return so we weren't only talking about me.

Soon enough, we reached a two-storey Victorian terraced house with beautiful floral awnings and peach panels. An older-looking man came out and stood under the porch, protecting himself from the rain. He was rubbing his hands together nervously. As I ran out of the rain to join him on the porch, he stood directly in front of me holding my shoulders and taking in every inch of my face. I could tell his eyes were starting to well up as he gave me a hug. His hug was full of warmth and a wave of gratitude rushed over me. I could have cried. I wasn't quite sure why. *Maybe because this is the man that potentially saved my mother's life? Our lives?*

'Katie-Kat,' he said almost in a whisper, his voice breaking, 'you look so much like your mother!' He stood there again, looking at me from head to toe now, then embraced me once more. This time he was shaking.

'Uncle Patrick, Mom has spoken so fondly of you,' I said, watching him smile as I spoke the words softly.

'Call me Pat, please,' I could tell he was trying to keep himself together, poised. 'Let's get out of the rain, shall we?' He held my hand and walked me inside, Alice already disappearing with my bags. It was strange that I didn't feel as nervous as I thought I would; it felt as if I was just visiting after a few years away, not that it was the first time I had met them. Alice appeared again, coming down from the steps.

'Follow me, I'll show you to your room to freshen up a bit, it would have been a long train ride for you,' I followed Alice into an extravagantly decorated double room, which smelt like rose petals.

'This is your room, Katelyn. Take your time, and when you're ready, come down for tea.' She went to leave and turned back around, 'We're so happy to have you here!' She closed the door behind her as she left the room to give me some privacy. I looked at my new home for the next few days, walking over to the window to see all the funny-shaped, old-fashioned-looking cars outside on the road. The streets were so different compared to New York City; it was greener, and people looked friendlier. I could hear Uncle Pat and Alice talking downstairs, so I had a quick shower and changed my clothes to feel a little more refreshed and comfortable.

'I hope she's not a vegetarian,' I heard Alice say as I was coming down the stairs. The creak of each wooden step signalled I was on my way down; by the last one, Alice had a tea ready for me.

'How're you feeling?' they both asked at the same time, ushering me to take a seat and relax on the sofa.

'I'm good, all this travelling is pretty tiring, especially after spending a week with two young Australians in a hostel dorm room!' I told them, taking a sip of the tea. Alice and Pat looked nervous now, like they had nothing to say. I took a sip of the tea. It was the best tea I had ever tasted.

'Biscuits?' Alice asked, pointing to a spread of food and sweets on the coffee table between us.

'No, this is perfect, thank you!'

The three of us talked all night. Uncle Pat told Alice stories of when he used to babysit me as a child, and how Mom used to tell him off for giving us candy. He seemed to only share the good stories, very few of my father. I knew he was considering my feelings, and yet I had so many questions to ask him about it, but I knew the time wasn't now.

'Mom told me that you used to travel a lot?' I asked.

'Oh, did she now?' he responded jovially. It was as if Mom was there in the room with us. I couldn't stop thinking about her.

'I've seen a fair bit. But that was many years ago now; I'm an old man, Katie, if you haven't already noticed! In fact, I always made sure to send things back for you kids.'

'Why did you move here? Why didn't you stay with us in New York?' I asked. *Have I taken it too far? Oh, Kate, what have you done?* Alice looked at Uncle Pat, with more curiousness than anything else, an uncomfortable silence where nobody knew what to say.

'Oh, you know, life just happened,' he said, deflecting. 'I was ready for a new adventure, and I had family here, most of my dad's side. It's very different here compared to New York, as I'm sure you'll soon discover.' I tried to stop a yawn from escaping but couldn't help it.

'It's late,' said Uncle Pat, 'we should call it a night.' He stood up and kissed us both goodnight on the cheek, taking our cups to the kitchen sink. I turned toward the stairs.

'Katelyn?'

'Yes?'

'I'm so very glad you're here, I've missed you all dearly.'

'I'm glad I came too, I'm sure Mom has missed you as well.' He nodded and continued his way to the kitchen, leaving me wondering what had happened all those years ago as I dragged my weary body to bed. As soon as my face touched the pillow, I was out like a light.

29

Alice

I woke up to the shrill sound of my mobile phone ringing. I didn't even know who it was when I picked up.

'Hello?' I barely got out, my voice rusty.

'Katelyn?' I knew his voice instantly. It was Mark.

'Mark?'

'Yes, it's me,' he responded. I went silent, not knowing what to say.

'How are you?' he continued.

'I'm good. How are you?'

'I'm okay,' he said, 'I miss you.' Again, the deathly silence filled the air between us. I didn't feel ready to return those words.

'Are you really coming here?'

'Do you still want me to?' he asked. I hesitated.

'I don't know, Mark. I want you to because I don't want to regret it one day if I say no.'

'I understand. I've booked my flight. Let's just see where this goes, okay?'

'Okay,' I responded, not feeling confident in what was going to unfold, the pit of my stomach almost bubbling.

'What time do you get in?' I asked.

'I'll email you the details.' A long pause followed. I took a deep breath and exhaled much louder than I'd anticipated.

'Katelyn, this is a good thing. This is good for us. I know it. Couples go through difficult times, before they, you know, really commit to each other. It's normal, healthy, even.'

I wanted to believe him, but I couldn't shake that something didn't feel right. 'We'll talk when you get here.'

'I just wanted to hear your voice before I saw you and double check it was still okay. I'll see you soon. I'll call you this time tomorrow.' *If he could see how unconvinced my face is, would he still get on the plane?*

'Bye, then.' We hung up, but I was still confused about when he would be here. *He said for my birthday, but he said he would call me tomorrow? Where is he going to stay?* I knew I wasn't going to stay in a hotel room with him after Uncle Pat and Alice kindly agreed to host me. I was still half asleep and didn't want to waste my morning in bed, so I put on loose clothes and made my way downstairs.

'Oh wow! What a spread!' I said, looking at all the food on the table. 'Urmm, which army do you plan on feeding?'

'I hope you're hungry!' Uncle Pat said, patting his large, round belly.

'How did you sleep, Katelyn?' Alice asked, while gesturing to see if I wanted coffee or tea. I pointed at the tea and winked.

'Perfect!' I said. 'Mark woke me up, actually; he just called.' Alice and Pat didn't budge from what they were doing.

'Your partner, right?' she asked, smiling like she had a plethora of questions coming my way that very second.

'Ah well, kind of,' I took a chair and turned it toward them both.

'How does it feel being so far from him, must be hard?' she began her dig.

'Well, we broke up before I left. He emailed me a couple of days ago about coming to visit, and I guess, to sort things out. It's a kind gesture, so I said yes, but I don't know.'

'Oh gosh, I'm sorry. I didn't know that. Are you okay with him coming here, then?'

'I don't know, it's a big thing for him to offer it, so I figure there's no harm to see where it goes?' Uncle Pat was in the room, but he didn't say anything. He didn't seem like the kind of person that would share his opinion; he seemed like someone who doesn't react and doesn't speak unless it made the conversation better.

'Hmm, yeah, I see your dilemma.' She smiled at me sympathetically. 'Well, I can't help you there, but I can give you haggis?' I scrunched my face and nodded out of sheer curiosity and a pinch of bravery. I put the smallest piece on my fork and took a modest bite. I spat it out quickly. *Well, at least I tried it.*

'Want more?' Alice asked, jokingly. This time I shook my head.

'So, we have loads of ideas for today …' she said. 'We thought we'd take you to see some family this morning, and then, if the weather holds out, we could hike up to Arthur's Seat. Dad will stay in the car for that part! We both have to work tomorrow but we'll give you a key and you can do as you please,' she paused, 'if that's okay with you?'

'Sounds perfect,' I said, grateful for all the effort they were making. I didn't know whether or not to tell them it was my birthday tomorrow. *Do I really want to spend it in another country alone?* I didn't, but I also didn't want them to take more time off work. It was just another birthday, after all.

'Maybe I could go to the castle tomorrow?' I suggested.

'That's a brilliant idea, I think it's a nice day tomorrow too.' I used to drag Mark to galleries and museums in New York, but he'd make me rush through them or he'd wait outside, which would take the excitement away. Now I could take my time exploring every nook and cranny of the castle if I wanted to. It was the perfect birthday present to myself.

After we'd eaten and cleaned up, Alice and I took a taxi into the city. Uncle Pat stayed at home, telling us he had some last-minute errands to tend to. We walked down her favourite cobblestone streets until we got to a quaint-looking house.

'This is where our Aunty Carol lives,' Alice said, while we walked down the stony path to the front door. Aunty Carol was waiting for us and opened the door excitedly. I could see similarities to my brother this time, something about the way her nose was slightly wider than mine and the way the corner of her lip curved up when she was amused. My brother did that when he didn't want to smile but his body couldn't stop it. She invited us in for tea and biscuits, and we spent a couple of hours looking through some old family albums, sharing stories. Carol had met Mom a few times when she went to visit Uncle Pat in New York. When we left a couple of hours later, Alice started leading us to somebody else's house.

'You know, as much as I love meeting the family, I'm exhausted,' I told Alice.

'Don't worry, Aunty Carol still does that to me,' she said, laughing; she could tell I wouldn't enjoy the next visit if we went.

'You aren't really getting to experience Edinburgh, are you?' she finally said. I didn't want to seem ungrateful, so didn't respond. 'Well, what DO you feel like doing?'

'Honestly, Alice. I don't need another tea – I need a *drink!*' I said, shrugging my shoulders.

'I know the perfect place!' She marched forward, linking her arm in mine, and a few minutes later, we were at a grey-brick pub with traditional music playing softly in the background. There were wooden tables and chairs, filled with locals.

'This is my favourite place!' she said, looking very pleased with herself. It felt cosy.

'There's a huge dog in here!' I said as soon as we walked in, pointing to a large labrador beneath a table.

'Yeah,' she said, 'aren't they allowed in pubs in New York?'

'I don't think so,' I said, making a face. 'Is that hygienic?' Alice ignored me, or didn't hear me, and pointed me to an empty round table before lining up at the bar. My eyes started spotting more and more dogs; there were probably eight altogether, some large and some little. They were all well-behaved. Luna would have loved it.

'I've let the family know we will be here for the rest of the evening, and to pop by as they please,' she informed me as she brought over our beers. It felt like a relief to not sit in anymore strangers' homes. I had a beer in my hand and my favourite cousin sitting next to me.

'Alice,' I said quietly while we were still alone, 'where is your mom?' She went silent and took a sip of her beer before she replied.

'Mom left us when I was quite young, I don't really remember her, and she never made contact. Dad doesn't really talk about it and doesn't seem to answer any of my questions.'

'Oh, wow, I'm sorry to hear that. My mom never mentioned it.'

'Honestly, she probably doesn't know. Uncle Pat never really spoke of your mom, and I don't like asking him questions about it. He always looks so uncomfortable when it's brought up. To be honest, as glad as he is that you're here, he was very hesitant at first.'

'I wonder why? Do you think it's to do with Mom?' We both went quiet, unsure of what it meant, or if it meant nothing at all. I changed the subject to something a little more exciting. 'So, Alice, is there someone special in your life?'

'Right now, afraid not. It's hard to find a man that doesn't spend all their time drinking in a place like this!'

'What about him?' I joked with her, pointing to the attractive barman in the distance.

'Gary?' Alice laughed and rolled her eyes, 'Oh, please, I grew up with him, he's about as mature as a seven-year-old child. He's practically a big brother!'

'That's a shame!' I winked. 'He's cute.'

'Do you wish Mark were here? Right here, right now?' she asked, changing the subject. We both seemed to be pretty good at that.

'I don't know. I mean, I miss having a go-to person to call. But we barely had sex, we barely did anything together. I don't know if I want that life anymore.' I looked down at my beer, wishing it would give me all the answers I needed.

'Well, it's impressive he's coming. I guess all you can do is see how it goes.'

Alice bought us more beers from the bar, and as she did, the relatives and family friends began to arrive. The afternoon soon drifted into evening, and it wasn't until they were closing that we realised just how late it was.

'New to the area?' the attractive barman asked as he wiped our tables down. He had a dark brown bristly beard and deep hazel eyes; he was wearing a checked shirt and worn jeans with an old baseball cap. He had a tea towel slung over his shoulder.

'Just visiting family,' I said, feeling my cheeks burn, hoping they weren't going red.

'Have you had the grand tour?' he asked, maintaining intense eye contact that I didn't want to break.

'Oh, stop it, Gary, she has a boyfriend!' Alice laughed, shaking her head, trying to take the attention away from me.

'Is that why you didn't introduce me, Alice? Where is he? I would love to meet the man who is lucky enough to have found this beautiful woman.' He took my hand and kissed it, winking. My cheeks burned a little deeper, surprised nobody else seemed bothered by his openly romantic gesture. *Does he always do this?*

'He's still in New York,' I stuttered, pulling my hand away from his and back onto my lap, trying to break the gaze.

'Well, then, happy to show you around if the lovely Alice over here has to work.' He took a pen from his shirt pocket and wrote his number on my left hand. Maybe I should've moved away, but I hadn't received attention like this since before Mark and I were together. His hands were warm, and he was holding mine firmly, goosebumps rising on my hands and chest.

'Okay, enough, Gary. We're off now. Better get her away from you,' Alice said, standing up and putting money on the table. I dug into my purse, but she shook her head and smacked my hand away. She was getting good at that.

'Thank you,' I said, shaking my head and smiling at her. Everyone at the table seemed to know Gary, shaking his hand or giving him a hug as they left the bar.

It was dark outside, and the air was crisp; everyone was running from the bar straight to their car, Uber or waiting for a taxi to pass. We waited for everyone else to leave, and as we saw a taxi pull up, Alice ran toward it, waving her hand to catch the driver's attention. I followed her, quickly – and almost involuntarily – looked back one more time. Gary was behind the bar, looking back, as if he was waiting for it. As I smiled, he lifted his cap ever so slightly and winked at me. If I wasn't red at the table, I was surely a shade of it now. The smile didn't leave my face as I ran to the taxi that Alice was now yelling from to hurry up. I didn't know if it was the cups of tea, the pints of beer or the crisp Scottish air, but I hadn't felt that invigorated in years.

30

Surprise

I woke up to a series of noises coming from downstairs. It sounded as if furniture was being rearranged, the scraping of chair legs being dragged against the wooden floors. *Why on earth would they be moving furniture? What time did Mark say he was calling?* As I reached for the phone, I saw Gary's faded number written on my hand. *Oh god. I'd forgotten all about that for a moment.* I tapped my phone to see the time – 9:27am. No missed calls or messages. Nothing. I opened Facebook and Instagram to see happy birthday messages from friends, family, my now ex-colleagues, noticing that Alice and Uncle Pat hadn't written anything yet. *Maybe they haven't seen it this morning?* I didn't respond to any of them, instead, I looked at Gary's number written across my hand, firstly concerned about the toxins that might be seeping into my body from the ink but then wondering how bad it would be if I did text him.

The alcohol fog began to set in from one too many beers the night before. Slowly moving to wash my face and wriggle into my Levi's and a black baggy knit, looking at the number on my hand with each movement. It was 10:00am when I finally left my room and made my way down the stairs.

'HAPPYYY BIIIRTTHDDAAYYYY!'

I froze. Startled. My left hand was on the staircase handrail, where my eyes were focused on Gary's number, then readjusted to face everyone standing downstairs.

'How di—' I started. 'Mark? Wha—?' He was the first person I saw in the crowd smiling at me.

'Well, I told you I'd speak to you around this time today, didn't I? Sorry I didn't call first like I said ...' He waited for a moment, 'So, do I get a hug? Or ...' I continued walking down the stairs slowly, now seeing the rest of my family, widening my eyes once they met Alice's.

'So, I guess you've all met Mark, then?' I laughed awkwardly, hugging all my family before getting to Mark. 'Remember, I've only told you great stuff about him.' I nudged him playfully. Mark embraced me and went in for a kiss, but I instinctively turned my cheek, not ready to completely pretend everything was okay when it wasn't.

'As much as we'd love to stay and spend your birthday with you, we have to go to work,' said Alice. I realised they had been waiting for Mark to get there and me to wake up.

'Of course! You guys didn't have to do this. Honestly.'

'We left the key on the table. I hope you guys have an amazing day! We thought we'd take you both to the pub tonight for dinner. Can you be ready for seven?'

'Perfect!' I said, hugging Alice. 'Thank you so much!' It was crazy to think that this time three months ago, I didn't even know the names or faces of these family members. I watched them all leave for work, thanking them as they left presents stacked on the entry table for me. Once everyone had left, the house fell silent. I looked at Mark.

'How?' I asked, not quite believing he was here, in Scotland, and away from the office. He seemed so confident, like it was almost one big joke. He pulled up a seat and ushered me to sit in it. My body was tense; I wasn't able to relax, not after how we'd left things in New York.

'Mark, we need to ta—' I started, before he cut me off.

'We will, let's just enjoy your birthday, and we can talk later.' I didn't want to pretend that everything was fine, but I also didn't want to argue on the day he flew in. I took a deep breath and relaxed while he handed me a coffee and brought a plate from the kitchen, my favourite: French toast with berries and maple syrup.

'Dig in!' His hands gestured to eat, while he got his own plate of eggs and bacon. We sat at the table opposite each other.

'How's Luna?' I asked softly.

'She's having a great time at your mom's, Derrick is in love,' he paused, and then added, 'she is actually the one that gave me the idea to come here. I called her to get your family's details just in case, and she said I should surprise you for your birthday. I want to take all the credit for it, but if it wasn't for her …' he trailed off. I wish Mom had warned me about this. 'What's that?' he asked, pointing to my hand.

'Oh, it's nothing, it's one of my cousin's numbers from last night and I haven't managed to get it off,' I lied. *Did I just lie to Mark about another man?* I wanted to tell him the truth, but I also didn't.

'Well, I wouldn't mind going to the castle today. Want to join me?' I asked, changing the subject. I knew Mark well enough to know that he wouldn't want to, but I was going to try my birthday luck anyway. He didn't say no, instead he changed the subject to work and then the house. It felt like he was verbally downloading everything he would have told me in the last few months that he didn't get a chance to. I wondered if he had spoken to anyone at home, if he hung out with his friends or lost himself in work once more. I listened on, making gestures or sounds that I was listening and the occasional 'oh yeah'. When I could feel conversation drying, I quickly interjected.

'I'm going to clean up and pack for the castle. Can you be ready in thirty minutes?'

'Can we go there tomorrow? I actually bought some lunchtime theatre tickets for the two of us.'

'Why would we go to a theatre at lunchtime? Isn't it more of an evening thing?' I asked.

'Well, it was a bit cheaper, and it gave us the morning to ourselves, and Alice already mentioned to me they wanted to do a dinner for you,' he said. *I guess it makes sense.*

'Okay, is it far? Can we walk?' I asked, grabbing my phone and opening my trusty maps app.

'What do you mean?' he laughed, 'Let's just taxi it. Why bother wasting time getting there?'

'The weather is nice for a change, and maybe we'll find a cute store or place to eat?' I started bargaining, trying to make a case for myself.

'I've already made reservations for lunch after the theatre, so we don't need to stumble across anything to eat.' I was taken aback by his responses, unsure if it always tended to be his way or if I was being hyper-sensitive at the moment.

'Fine,' I folded, 'what do you want to do in the meantime?' I asked.

'I don't know, what is there to do? Doesn't seem like there's much around here?' I found this, too, triggering.

'Well, I guess we don't have time for much else if we're going to a lunchtime show anyway?' I responded, my energy feeling like it was seeping away from me.

'You're right. I'll unpack my things upstairs and freshen up,' he gave me a kiss on the lips and took his things upstairs to my room, following the direction he saw me coming from this morning. I collapsed on the couch, closed my eyes and took a big breath. *Is this what the rest of the trip is going to be like?* I heard my phone ring from the kitchen table. It was Alice.

'Hey, Katelyn, have you left for the castle yet? I heard they have some special event happening there today!' she said, sounding excited. *Oh, great.*

'No, Mark booked us to see some lunch show,' I said glumly.

'A matinee? Well, you'll be there with all of Edinburgh's geriatrics!' she sounded amused.

'I don't want to talk about it,'

'Bugger! Never mind, I'll see you tonight and we'll have lots of fun,' she said, 'I promise, Katie.' I didn't even know what the event was, but I couldn't believe I was missing it. *Maybe I could get him to change his mind?*

'Maarrrkkk?' I bellowed from downstairs, half-standing and half-kneeling on the couch. 'Alice called to say there's some cool event happening at the castle today.'

'Did you tell her I already bought tickets for the show?' he asked, walking down the stairs, not one to raise his voice.

'Yes, but she said this might be better,' I told him, hoping he'd ask me what I wanted to do … for my birthday.

'What if it starts raining and we're outside?' he sat on the couch opposite me, clearly not open to the suggestion. I guess that was my answer. *Sigh*. I lay back down on the couch and stared at my hand, the numbers barely visible. I saved them in my phone as *Gary Bar*.

I didn't say much during the taxi ride to the theatre and Mark wasn't pleased with me after it.

'Kate?' he nudged part way through the show. I looked up abruptly. 'What?'

'You started snoring!' he said firmly, looking annoyed.

'I didn't, did I?' I tried to hold back a laugh. I couldn't help nodding off, it didn't hold my attention. We took another taxi to lunch, passing all the beautiful cobblestone streets we could have been walking down, passing all the stores we could have popped into for no reason. The taxi stopped at an upper-class, fancy restaurant. It was dimly lit, and a huge wooden shelf of very expensive international wines took up the entire length of the wall. It was beautiful. We were taken to our seats, a candle lit, handed menus, and before we'd even had a chance to sit down, I ordered a martini.

'Don't you want a nice wine?' Mark asked.

'No, I want a cocktail.'

'Certainly. And for you, sir?' the waiter asked politely.

'I'll have a glass of the malbec.' Mark responded.

'This is a beautiful place.' I said, still looking around in amazement by the high ceilings and glass decor around the room.

'Are you sure you're enjoying yourself?' he asked. I sensed a nasty undertone.

'So, tell me about your flight over?'

'It was fine; it was long, and the food was horrible.'

'Sit next to any crazies?' I said, thinking about Quella.

'I didn't really talk to anyone,' he responded. Our conversation didn't flow, and it surprised me, with so much time apart, we seemingly had nothing to talk about.

'When I flew to Iceland, I sat next to this woman, Quella. I found her so intimidating at first but ended up staying with her and her husband, and it was the best experience,' I said, for the first time bringing up my travels even though he didn't ask.

'Don't you think that's a bit irresponsible?'

'I'm not going to lie, it was a bit daunting at first, but I found that everyone I met was incredibly trustworthy – I even met two Australian girls that I then travelled to London with.' Mark didn't seem interested. *Is he jealous? Or maybe he truly doesn't understand?*

'You seem … different?' he said. I nearly choked on my martini as I took another sip.

'I think I am,' I responded. 'I think leaving New York was the best thing I ever did.'

'It's not real, though?' he said, frustrated. 'This is not normal life, it's an escape from it.'

'I'm not having this conversation with you, Mark. I've been having the time of my life, and right now, on my birthday, on a day I had already planned and was looking forward to, you come and ruin everything. You didn't even have the audacity to ask me what I wanted to do today, and now you're telling me I am living a fantasy.' I excused myself and went to the bathroom, to calm down and stop myself from saying something I may regret. When I got back to the table, our mains were there, and another martini.

'I'm sorry. Why didn't you say that before?' asked Mark. It slowly dawned on me that, for the last eight years, I folded to whatever Mark wanted. I never truly told him what *I* wanted or needed.

'I thought it might start an argument and I'd seem ungrateful given you have travelled all the way here for me,' I said, playing with my food with my fork.

'I don't know things you don't tell me.' I didn't know how genuine he was being, but he was right. I didn't share with him what I wanted to do to avoid an argument, and I needed to be honest about what I was feeling if this was ever going to work. 'It will get better, Katie. I promise.'

31

Birthday

When we got to the bar just before 7pm, Alice and Uncle Pat were the only ones there. Uncle Pat and Mark went together to organise drinks and food.

'So, how was the show?' Alice asked, moving close to me, voice slightly hushed.

'I fell asleep,' I groaned, my face frowning.

'Give him credit for the thought, I guess.'

'I know, I have. It's hard. Having been apart all this time. And then seeing him again as a surprise I was not mentally prepared for. I feel different.'

'I know, I'm sorry I didn't tell you. I promised him. How've things been otherwise?' she asked, genuinely concerned.

'It's strange, it kind of feels forced and fake, like I'm putting on a show … I'm sure after a bit of time it'll get better.' Alice gave my arm squeeze as Mark and Uncle Pat returned to the table. Then I heard it. That thick, deep Scottish accent. My left hand that was on the table moved to my lap in an attempt to hide it while butterflies set into my stomach.

'Happy birthday, Katie-Koo!' Gary said. His voice was buttery. This time the tea towel was tucked into his jeans.

'Oh, thanks, Gary. Gary, this is my partner Mark, he flew in from New York last night to surprise me!'

'Nice to meet you, Mark,' he said, holding his arm out to shake his hand.

'You too, Gary,' Mark responded politely, shaking it in return.

'What did you get up to today, birthday girl?' he asked, turning back to me.

'Mark bought tickets to a show.'

'Oh lord, are you sixty?' he asked cheekily. 'No, I hear they're great, I can't seem to sit still for such a long time, though!'

'Oh no, it was really good!' I lied, glancing at Mark. Alice looked at me, then pretended to read the menu.

'I'm glad you enjoyed it, love,' he paused for a moment, then continued, 'well, then, what can I get for ya?' he asked.

'Oh, Pat and I have ordered for the table already.' Mark interrupted, but as he said it, the rest of the family entered the bar and headed over to us. Once more, shaking Gary's hand or patting him on the back, whatever their personal hello was to him. Alice could tell how uncomfortable Mark and I were looking.

'Beers for all, and check on our food order, please, Gaz,' Alice jumped in. Gary nodded, taking all the menus off the table. As I handed the one in front of me to him, he spotted his number on my hand. He chuckled. *I should've scrubbed harder.* I didn't know if Mark had noticed, but I refused to look at him to find out.

All night, I kept myself from looking at Gary but could sense when he was near our table; I knew if he was looking at me from the bar or when he brushed against me handing out drinks or food. I could smell his cologne when he got near; I could hear his voice in the distance. The entire evening, I was thinking about the next time he would be close to me again. I felt like a little girl that had a crush that I wasn't allowed to have.

Once we got home, Mark went straight upstairs, no thank yous or goodnights. He got ready for bed in silence and didn't even acknowledge or look at me once. As soon as I climbed into bed beside him, it began – what I had been dreading since he got here.

'That number on your hand, it's Gary's, isn't it?' he accused.

'Yes,' I answered him quietly, and this time, truthfully.

'Why didn't you tell me the truth when I asked you?' a mixture of anger and disappointment in his voice.

'I didn't want to make you feel uncomfortable, and I didn't feel I owed you an explanation. We are not together, Mark!'

He seemed surprised by my response, taking a minute to digest it. 'What happened the night he wrote his number?'

I sighed, frustrated, but also not really knowing what to say. 'The night before you arrived, we all went to the pub and that was when we met. He seems to be a family friend of everybody's, Mark. You saw them all today. He just told me to call him if I needed anything.'

'So, instead of warning me about his little crush on you, I had to watch him flirt with you all night and figure it out for myself?' his voice sounded angrier and louder now; I knew that Uncle Pat and Alice were listening to everything.

'Mark, please don't. I barely spoke to him tonight, just like the night before when I met him.' I had never before seen such jealousy in his eyes. But Mark wasn't done.

'Are there any other guys on your trip I should know about?' he asked.

'We aren't together, Mark,' I said stubbornly. As I leant over to turn off the bedside lamp, he pulled out a card and threw it at me.

'Then who's this? Who's Christian?' he demanded, staring me dead in the eye. His eyes were dark, cold. I had never seen him like this before. I had never stared at his face close enough, for long enough, to see the wrinkles that crawled their way to each corner of his eyes as he frowned.

'Where did you even find that?'

'Who's Christian?!' he asked again, deflecting my curiousness as to whether he had been going through my things.

'He sat next to me on the plane. He liked my photos,' I responded.

'I doubt it was the photos he liked,' Mark said sarcastically, rolling his eyes. I could feel the heat rise in my skin, a tingling sensation down my back through to my fingertips. I didn't want to lie in this bed with him. We sat in silence for a few minutes. I made a conscious effort to steady my breath with closed eyes. *Stay calm. Be patient.*

I wondered if the reason I had never seen this side of Mark was because I had never stepped out of line before. I didn't go out often with friends, I didn't stay out late or do things he didn't approve of. I always tried to be the epitome of what a good woman was supposed to be. *Where is the 'yes' person that was always so scared of hurting people or saying the wrong thing?* I didn't know. I didn't think she was there anymore.

'Look, nothing has happened on this trip, and you need to trust that I'm telling you the truth,' I moved across the bed toward him, rubbing his back to offer comfort in this foreign place that he travelled to for hours to see me for my birthday.

'Mark, I—' I began, but he kissed me on the lips instead.

'I'm sorry,' he said, kissing me again. I tried to relax into it. He kissed my chin, then my neck.

'Mark, I can't. I can't act like nothing has happened with us. I can't pretend you did't let me move out of our home after eight years of being together.'

'I miss you,' is all he could muster up.

'That's not enough, Mark. What did you expect from this trip?'

'I want you in my life, Katelyn. It's empty without you. All I know is I want you.'

A few months ago, it would have been all I needed to hear. He kissed me again and I kissed him back, we lay in bed entwined in each other's arms, but he didn't feel like home anymore. I tried to relax again, waiting for my body to respond to his touch like it should have. It didn't. I found my thoughts wandering to those deep brown eyes. Maybe I should have stopped, maybe it wasn't right to think of someone else, but I didn't want to stop. I wanted to feel wanted again.

32

Gary

Somehow, Mark and I managed to get through the next few days without fighting – partly because we kept conversation shallow. Mark was working remotely, and I continued exploring Scotland, keeping him informed or inviting him along if I thought he would like it. The few things he came to, I'd stroll on ahead and take photos, focusing on the techniques that Janine taught me, with Christian's seed of selling my prints planted firmly in my mind. We seemed on autopilot, our hugs and kisses felt generic and lifeless, but it was better than the emotional roller-coaster we went on that first day. I didn't know if anyone had noticed the tension mounting between us. I had gotten to a point where I would check his calendar in the morning for meetings, and the ones with a subject line in capital letters, I knew were important so I couldn't speak to him in that time.

With the sun making rare appearances, I would make time to go for short strolls around the neighbourhood and enjoy it, taking my camera with me and doing nothing in particular.

'AMERICA!' I heard someone yell. I looked around. I couldn't shake the infectious smile that I caught. Gary pulled up at the end of the street and started yelling out of the car window.

'Scotland,' I said under my breath, walking toward his car ever so casually, like my heart wasn't racing and butterflies weren't fluttering around in my belly.

'Get in!' he said, waving his hand frantically.

'I'm fine, thanks, I have to get back,' I told him sheepishly, reminding him that I was travelling with Mark.

'Oh, relax, I know you're a married woman,' he said, rolling his eyes. 'I just noticed you and your camera and wanted to show you something.' He waited for a moment and then continued, 'I'll bring you home soon, and I promise I won't try it on with you. I'm a gentleman, your family know,' he paused for a moment, 'shall we invite Mark, then?' he asked, nodding his head toward Alice and Uncle Pat's house.

'He has important meetings today.' Gary didn't look surprised. 'Where is this place, anyway?'

'Well, that's for you to find out, isn't it? Come on an adventure?' he said, as he started revving the engine playfully. I rolled my eyes and got in the car. I'd seen the way he was around my family and knew there was nothing to worry about. He drove for some time, sharing interesting facts about places we were passing and old folktales that I didn't know if he was making up on the spot. After about twenty minutes of luscious hilly scenery, we arrived at a stunning ravine. It was so many different shades of green, reds and oranges, with gravel roads and sheep in the paddocks. Besides a few cars in the distance and the birds chirping, it was silent. And we were alone. Gary turned off the engine and we got out of the car, both appreciating the serenity. It reminded me of how Quella and I walked around the waterfalls in Iceland, neither of us needing to talk to enjoy each other's company. It felt comfortable. Here I was, again, another perfect stranger in another unforgettable moment.

'I don't know if you see this very often, being a New York gal,' he explained. 'My mother lives close by, but this is my favourite part of the drive.' He pointed to the rolling hills in the distance, but I could feel him looking at me – he was very close. I didn't meet his eyes, I took photos instead.

Click click click. I photographed everything. The depth of the field mesmerised me, the hills looked so close; the tranquil spot only minutes from the town I had been staying in. *I could get used to this.* I heard the car moving, but stopped myself turning around. I didn't want to seem too interested in what he was doing. When I finally looked over, I saw him lying on the roof of the car. The light of the sunset created a perfect silhouette, illuminating his body. He wasn't looking my way, he was lying on his back gazing up at the sky, his elbows open, resting his head in his palms. I clicked away. When I captured enough, I pulled myself up on the roof and lay next to him.

'You are lucky, you know, to live here like this. So simply,' I said. Gary was silent for a moment; he was choosing his words.

'You only think I'm lucky because it's different to what you have. You could live like this too, you choose not to,' he said, not rudely nor bluntly.

'I can't pick up and move everything to Scotland!'

'That's not what I meant,' he said. 'You could live in New York where it's green and hilly. You could live in simplicity out of the city,' he said. I didn't say anything. He was right. 'My parents always tell me I could do so much more, but I'm perfectly happy. I work, I have money to buy what I want, I have time for all the people I love,' he laughed and then continued, 'while people like Mark are missing out on special moments like this. But for what? To earn more money to afford a first-class plane ticket to Scotland, to only sit in a house and work more? That's not my idea of happiness. But, hey, that's just me, and we need all types of people in this world.'

'You don't think that's a little judgemental?'

'I don't mean to judge. I sense your unhappiness when you're with him. Two people should complement each other, not only exist together.'

'I'm not unhappy,' I said, focusing on only that small part of what he said.

'You were happy the first night I met you – you were glowing. I didn't see that glow on your birthday, of all days.'

'This trip has been a big change for me, I quit my job to travel, and Mark and I separated not long ago. I feel like I don't know anything anymore,' I shared, not knowing why I was baring my soul to this man I didn't even know.

'Well, you must know what makes you unhappy. Maybe he has changed, maybe you have. Maybe your lives were meant to cross paths to teach each other something, maybe that lesson has been taught, or maybe it hasn't.' I lay there, absorbing everything he'd said. I turned to look at him, our faces close, the golden hour sun heating our exposed skin. 'I told you I wasn't going to try it on with you and that I was a gentleman,' he reminded me, almost whispering. I closed my eyes and felt my entire body tingle.

'It feels like I've known you a long time,' I said, turning to face the sky, breaking the intensity I know we both felt.

'Katelyn?' he said, slowly leaning over toward me, making my heart beat faster and my breath quicken.

'Yes?' I whispered back, matching the softness in his voice, terrified he was going to kiss me but wondering if I would stop him if he did.

'As much as I want to stay, we need to move along to our next destination.' The tension between us evaporated as he sat up and carefully slid down the back window and jumped off the boot.

'Next destination?' I repeated. He helped me down and we got into the car. He fired up the engine and we were off.

'Where're we going?' I asked.

'Stop with the questions, lady. It wouldn't hurt to have a few surprises in your life.' I was taken aback but amused at the same time.

I listened to the local radio as I watched the sun set while he continued to drive. He pulled up onto a steep driveway, where a red-brick terraced house stood behind a luscious green garden. I didn't ask where we were; I got out of the car and followed him along the stony path. He took my hand and directed me to the front door. A short, round woman with a floral dress opened it quickly, smiling from ear to ear as she embraced Gary.

'And you must be Katelyn!' she said, unexpectedly hugging me too.

'Come in, come in!'

'Your mom?' I turned to ask him, amused and bemused.

'Sit down, dinner is ready, Gary's always so punctual when food's concerned!' she said endearingly. Gary raised his eyebrows and nodded in agreement. She poured me a large glass of wine and asked me questions about America.

'Have you been to the Mets? I always wanted to go. My brother used to follow American baseball religiously.'

As I went to reply, Gary looked at me once more, pointing his fingers to the front door.

'Mam, I'm sorry, but I have one more stop for Cinderella here before she turns into a pumpkin.' His mom shook her head in humour.

'I'll see you this time next week, darling boy.' She packed a container of food for him, and he lovingly planted a kiss on her forehead. Together we made our way back to the car with full bellies and cups.

'Another stop?' I asked, walking to the passenger side of the car again.

'No, no. We can walk,' he said, leading me down the cobblestone streets, still holding the container of food. In a matter of minutes, we found ourselves at the front door of a pub that I'd somehow managed to completely miss on the drive to his mom's.

'Have you been to a ceilidh before?' he asked.

'No, I haven't!' I said, my eyes widening with excitement. We hung up our coats and took a seat at the corner table. Mark gestured for the barman, and without any words exchanged, two pints came out instantly.

He swapped the container of food for the beers and shook the barman's hand. The barman winked at me and walked away.

'Who was that?' I asked.

'The owner of the joint, we grew up together and to this day he still loves Mam's food.' Gary must've known the time the show began, because three sips of beer down and everyone started to cheer as the show commenced. The music made my ears ring and the whole crowd was clapping and cheering merrily. Everyone was up dancing, swinging each other around and swapping partners with every step.

Click click click. I didn't care about technique this time. One of the dancers pulled Gary onto the stage. As he was being dragged to the front, he gave my camera to the barman and grabbed my waist, pulling me in too. No-one cared how anyone else looked, we all danced our hearts out to the beat of the music. When the show was over and the pints were dry, the punters started clearing the pub. Gary looked at the time.

'Guess I better take you back, Cinderella, huh?' he said.

'Oh gosh, yes!' I said, looking at the time and realising I had not once messaged Mark. I checked my phone. It was 9pm.

'Is this your typical Monday night?' I asked.

'It sure is.'

'It's perfect!' Gary didn't say anything as we walked back to the car. We sat in silence for most of the drive home.

'So, you're off soon, eh?' he said as he pulled onto Alice's driveway, endorphins circulating through my body slowly decreasing and anxiety creeping in instead.

'I think so. I'm still a bit undecided,' I said, looking down, wishing I spent more time with him.

'Life will treat you well, America. Make decisions for you, not for others. If you follow the direction of your smile, you can't go wrong.' I opened my car door and turned back to face him.

'I feel like this is the last time I'll see you,' I said.

He gave me a hug and whispered, 'It feels like I've known you forever too.' I took a deep breath, confused by how emotional I was getting. I thanked him again as I got out of the car, wondering if our paths would ever cross again.

33

Trouble

When I walked through the front door, I had hoped to all the gods I could think of that Mark was asleep. He was sitting in the lounge room. Before he spoke, I did.

'Gary saw me walking on his way to his mom's, so we had dinner at her place and then went to a local pub for a pint and dancing.'

'And you didn't think to let me know where you were?'

'I know, I know. I'm sorry, it slipped my mind. He took me to a ceilidh and there was dancing, it was so much fun and time went so quickly.'

'A what?'

'A traditional Scottish dance.' Mark rolled his eyes in disbelief. 'It was amazing, Mark, you have to see the photos.' My nervousness subsided as I talked about the night and pulled out my camera, ready to show him some images.

'What did he whisper in your ear?' he asked sternly, refusing to end the conversation about Gary or looking at what I was trying to show him.

'He told me you were a lucky man,' I lied, shoving my camera in front of him so he could see the dance I was talking about.

'Well, I guess it was good of the guy to show you around,' Mark finally said, unconvincingly.

'Yes, it was very nice of him. I hope he wasn't late for work,' I regrettably said.

'I mean, he's a bartender, it's not even a real job,' he spat. I looked at him, surprised by his nasty words.

'Who are you to judge him? You barely know him.'

'I'm just saying, it's not like he has a serious career. Who would care if he was late?' Mark continued, 'Why do you care so much, anyway?'

'Because he's my friend, Mark. He is a good person that hasn't done anything wrong. What makes you so special? Money? So you can buy a first-class plane ticket to Scotland only to work? Please.' I started to walk up the stairs as Alice opened the hallway door.

'Hi, guys, everything okay?' she asked timidly.

'Yeah, things are fine.' Mark answered, walking past her and going upstairs. Alice gave me a look of concern, and my eyes began welling up.

'Let's go make a cuppa,' she said softly, nodding her head toward the kitchen. I followed behind her.

'Tea? Whisky?' she asked. I told Alice about everything – about how Mark had made me feel since being there, about the night with Gary.

'I knew something was going on, but I didn't want to pry,' she said.

'Was it bad that I went out with Gary today?' I asked.

'That's not a question for me to answer, Katie, you have to talk to Mark. How would you feel if the roles were reversed?' she asked me. *How would I have felt?* I know I wouldn't have liked him spending time with another woman I didn't know, but I wouldn't have neglected him in the first place if the roles were reversed. *Right?*

'I don't know. I feel as if I barely know Mark anymore, or maybe I'm only getting to know him now, and I don't like it.'

'Or maybe you're getting to know yourself more and it's all part of the growing pains,' Alice said, raising her eyebrows at me and shrugging her shoulders.

'I'm sorry. I'm sorry to bring all this drama into your home.'

Alice laughed. 'Please, I've seen much worse!' she said, while filling my glass with more Drambuie.

'Go on, go and have a chat with him, clear the air.'

I sighed, not wanting to have another uncomfortable conversation but knowing I had to. I shot back the last of my whisky. 'Wish me luck.' If the creaking staircase wasn't enough of a warning for Mark, the door was. I opened it slowly, and as I walked in, Mark was sitting in bed hunched over his laptop, a sight I was used to seeing.

'Mark?' I said softly, in a tone to tell him all guns were down and I was waving a white flag. As I got closer, I noticed he was holding two pieces of paper. 'Are you okay?' I asked.

'I bought these two tickets to Hawaii, I knew that was your next destination and hoped we could go there before we headed home.' I didn't know what to say. 'Do you even want to go with me?'

'I think this has been a big change for both of us,' is all I could muster up.

'I realise that with everything that's happened, and being with your family, we haven't had time for just you and me. Maybe that's what we need?' he pleaded.

'It's been a pretty intense few days, with you meeting my family and us trying to make it work,' I said, hoping the reassurance made him feel better.

'I think this trip will be good for us, and I promise to work a little less. I love you.'

'I love you too,' I repeated, feeling like we had remastered the three words that made everything appear better again.

34

Oahu

I didn't know what Hawaii would bring for Mark and me, but without Gary and my family around, I hoped things would be better between us. Mark was up two hours early to make sure we were both packed and ready. It was nice to have somebody else organising the various aspects of travelling, rather than having the pressure of doing it all myself. It allowed me extra time to spend with Alice and Uncle Pat, so I couldn't complain.

'Keep in touch, Kate,' Uncle Pat said as he gave me one of his bear hugs. 'And please send my love to your mom.' I turned to Alice, and all of a sudden the floodgates opened. I couldn't stop the tears falling from my eyes, drenching her shoulder. She was more than a cousin to me. She'd been my support and rock over the past few weeks, she was more like a sister to me.

'Thank you so much for everything,' I said softly in her ear, not wanting to leave her.

'Don't be a stranger, Katie. It's been our pleasure having you stay here. We'll miss you,' she said, holding me even tighter. Alice turned towards Mark, who was pacing beside the taxi looking at the time. We both couldn't help but chuckle.

'Time doesn't move any faster staring at the clock, you know?' I joked. He wasn't impressed. Alice squeezed my arm as we walked to the taxi, helping with my bags. We said our final goodbyes and were off. *Now it is just the two of us.*

Mark was on edge all the way to the airport, while I chatted away to the driver, impressed with how comfortable I had become talking to strangers now. I would have never done that in Manhattan. After a twenty-minute journey, we finally reached the airport. As I was getting out of the car and thanking the driver, I noticed Mark still fixated with his phone. He'd spent the entire car ride responding to work emails and making calls.

'You aren't going to do this all trip, are you?' I asked, clearly displaying my annoyance. It felt strange being at the airport with him. I instinctively started rolling my bags inside, checking which gate we needed to be at and making my way there. I was proud at how confident I had gotten with the process. I didn't know if Mark would be impressed by my independence or feel emasculated.

'Want to look at some of my photos?' I asked Mark once we found seats to get comfortable in until it was time to board.

'Not now, I'm doing as much as I can so I can relax on the trip,' he responded.

It was nice to wander around the airport without all my bags; it was also nice to sit business class on the flight. Mark wasn't interested in flying economy, waiting in lines or getting below-average food.

After what felt like forever, we finally arrived in Honolulu, on the island of Oahu. My eyes glued to the window to watch the descent – it was breathtaking, with the glistening turquoise ocean and shimmering white sand.

'Gosh, the world is so beautiful,' I said in a trance. As soon as we got off the plane, I could feel the island humidity, and I was excited after the cold in Manhattan, Iceland, London and Scotland. I couldn't wait to put on a bikini and hit Waikiki Beach, lay in the sand and soak in the sun.

We took a taxi to the five-star resort Mark had booked and checked into a room that had a balcony right overlooking the horizon.

'I'm heading straight to the beach!' I yelled to Mark from the bedroom, ripping my clothes off and foraging through my suitcase for the first bikini I could find.

'Aren't you hungry?' he asked.

'Nope, no way I'm going to bloat in this little number,' I had my bikini on already, grabbing the perfectly rolled beach towel from the perfectly made bed.

'I don't think we should do different things, how will I find you?' he asked.

'Okay, well, put on your swimming things, and we'll get food on the way to the beach, yeah?'

'I could eat and then come back and cha—' he started saying, but I cut him off. My patience felt worn.

'Nope, that's us meeting in the middle if you want me to come with you to get food!' Mark looked annoyed but made his way to his suitcase and started getting ready for the beach too. I was surprised he listened. It turned out Mark didn't like the ocean, or the sand, nor did he want to hike up any mountains or visit a pineapple plantation. I had no idea what he'd planned to do in Hawaii, and this new, confident version of myself wasn't going to let him stop me from experiencing Oahu the way I wanted to.

I booked tours through the resort, and a friend I met on the tour hired a car with me to visit the pineapple plantation where we also went to look at the Pipeline, watching world-class surfers and bodyboarders dance on the incredibly terrifying giant waves. I had a freaking ball.

'Do you have to talk to everyone you meet?' Mark said one evening over dinner, as I waved to a couple I went snorkelling with the day before.

'That's Kath and Steve, they are so lovely,' I responded instead, not letting his passive-aggressiveness penetrate the happiness and fulfilment I was feeling. I felt the same way I felt in Iceland and London – free.

35

Different

We continued for a few days with this unusual dynamic, me spending time away from the hotel room, and Mark sleeping in, connecting to his life in New York through social media or work or lying by the hotel pool drinking cocktails by himself. I joined him every second day, feeling obliged to make sure he didn't feel lonely or left out. Nothing actually changed from being on our own in Hawaii, to being with my family in Scotland – we only found other things to blame. Mark wasn't involving himself in what I enjoyed doing and there wasn't a happy balance. We were both growing increasingly impatient and frustrated with each other.

One evening, I went down ahead of him for dinner and decided to take my camera with me. I was taking pictures of the island dancers that were performing in the alfresco area of the restaurant when a gentleman by the bar approached me.

'Nice camera,' he said, looking at it.

'Thank you, it's been on some wonderful adventures with me recently,' I gushed, somehow getting onto the topic of Iceland.

'Oh, wow, I haven't been there before. Are you travelling for work?' he asked.

'No, I'm here holidaying with my partner,' I told him.

'Honeymooners?' he asked inquisitively.

'Nope, we're not married. I'm basically having a midlife crisis, and he's here to support me,' I joked, wondering how true that might have been.

'John,' he said, holding out his hand to introduce himself.

'Nice to meet you. I'm Katelyn,' I said, shaking it politely in return. John looked like he was in his forties, quite a fit stature with a grey beard and grey hair, neatly combed back. He was wearing a blue floral shirt and cargo shorts, holding a pina colada with an umbrella in it.

'How long have you been using it for?' he asked.

'Gosh, a month or so, max? My parents bought it for me before I left for Iceland.' John nodded. 'Are you a photographer?' I asked, keenly aware of how interested he was in the camera.

'I'm an artist. I came here on a holiday a few years ago and never left. How could you leave this?' he asked, leaning against the bar and looking out at the never-ending ocean, where the horizon had begun changing to shades of orange as the sun was setting.

'It amazes me how people manage that. I met a lady in Iceland that couldn't leave there as well. What do you do for money at first? How do you leave your home?' I was genuinely curious, feeling they were the main reasons I needed to go back home soon.

'I paint and sell my work in my store and online,' he said, like it was the simplest thing to do. I looked down at my camera. The screen showed a picture of one of the women dancing, focusing on her eyes just as they had closed to feel the music, sun setting in the background.

'Well, you would know then,' I handed him my camera. 'Would this sell?' I asked, sheepishly revealing the photo I had taken. I watched him as he studied it.

'It's a great photo. I can't promise you anything, but the quality and originality is there,' he said carefully, handing it back.

'I wish I could stay here,' I sighed, taking the camera back and now leaning onto the bar, both of us taking in the sunset, the girls still dancing.

'You could, if you really wanted to,' he said, followed by asking me what I did for work.

'Finance.' John and I both laughed at the absurdity of what I do for money, versus what I clearly felt passionate for.

'Oh, I felt passion in those words. You must love it,' he said smugly, taking a sip from his cocktail.

'It pays the bills.'

'So do a lot of things!' he said. 'The world is your oyster, young one.' He went on to share that some people have a spark, and for those people that feel it, it's important to follow it. 'This life wasn't made for everyone, though,' he added. I looked down with a mixture of feelings, unsure if I had the spark, and if I had it, why didn't I have the courage to follow it. I noticed John watching something behind me, so I turned around, feeling a rush of energy.

'Mark,' Mark said, as he held out his hand introducing himself to this unknown man talking to me. His chest was out, and John and I both felt stiffness in the air surrounding us.

'Ahhh, this must be the boyfriend,' John said, shaking his hand in return, remaining gentle and courteous. 'I was just telling your lovely lady how important it is to follow dreams.'

'I couldn't agree with you more,' Mark said, kissing me on the forehead. He was standing unusually close to me, like he was protecting me, or maybe trying to show his ownership of me – his dominance.

'You are with quite the photographer,' he continued, nodding his head toward me, making me blush as I held my camera tighter.

'She isn't an actual photographer, it's just a little hobby.' As Mark responded, I could feel heat engulf my entire body, a poignant and pungent taste overriding the sweetness of the pina colada that John ordered for me, but I stood there smiling respectfully.

'Well, I think her shots are phenomenal,' John said, clearly seeing through my smile and trying to ease the tension however he could. Mark nodded, not agreeing with John but marking the end of the conversation and getting the attention of the bartender to bring him a drink.

'Well, Katelyn, good luck with everything! Feel free to come by the art studio to check it out if you have some free time while you're here,' he said, getting a business card from his pocket and purposely placing it on the bar before walking away.

The dancers were now packing up, and the sun had set. The restaurant was lighting candles at all the tables. I looked at Mark, who had begun walking to an empty table, devastated he couldn't actually comment on whether or not he liked my work as he had never taken the time to look at it – not back in university, and still not to this day. *Is he truly oblivious to how little interest he shows in it? Or me? Or how much those words have hurt me?*

36

Changes

After that night by the bar, I felt like a part of me had disappeared, though I couldn't figure out what part it was or how to bring it back. I no longer felt inspired, empowered or independent. It had been replaced with confusion, doubt and obedience. Mark didn't seem to notice the change, or if he did, it made him feel more comfortable. I laid low. I stopped saying hello to people I had met on the tours, I stayed in the room and kept to myself. I stopped taking photos.

'Finally getting bored of taking pictures, huh?' Mark said one night at dinner, a strange tone of accomplishment in his voice. Like he had won, and I had lost. Like he was stronger, and I was weaker.

'No, I think I've captured enough on this trip,' I said, with little expression, playing with the food on my plate.

'Yeah, it's been a long trip. I'm ready to get back, that's for sure,' he replied, sitting high in his chair. I didn't respond, I didn't make eye contact. I stared at my plate.

'Have you missed home?' he asked, the most conversation he had made with me.

'I've missed Luna ... and the family,' I sighed. *Maybe I am feeling this way because I'm homesick?* 'I need to start thinking about what I'm going to do if I go back.'

'Well, you don't have to worry about finding a job when you're home,' he said, taking my hand. He had an amused look on his face, which made something at the pit of my stomach churn. I already knew I wasn't going to like what he was about to say. 'Before I left, I called Eileen and told her you'd been going through a few things. She was very sympathetic, and it seems they've missed having you around. I asked if you could have your job back when you return. And, Katie, she said you could have your job back. All this leave would be unpaid, of course!' I stared, unsure if he was being serious or not. While I may have not been thinking consciously since the moment with John and Mark before dinner a few nights ago, there must have been something bigger at play in my subconscious. As the words were leaving Mark's mouth, the hairs on the back of my neck rose and I started to tense, heat rising throughout my entire body once more. I could feel my heart rate increase, pumping blood faster than usual. I moved my hand away from his and sat up straight in my seat.

'You did what?' I responded, wanting to make sure I'd heard him correctly. Mark looked confused.

'You mean, thank you?' he asked, surprised by my reaction.

'I don't want to go back there, Mark.' I could feel my eyes tearing up, not from sadness but frustration. It was like as much as I tried to make it work and fit myself into this neat box I thought I should be in, the box was getting smaller, and I could no longer contain myself within it.

'What do you mean? You don't know how to do anything else,' he said, and with a smirk added, 'what else would you do? Take photos?'

'What if I do want to become a photographer? What if I am that good?' I said, feeling the part of me that had disappeared come back in full force, albeit through tears and uncertainty.

'Come on, Katie, you know that's not a real career.' I wanted so badly make a scene, yell and let it all out, but instead, I took a sip of water while I gathered my thoughts.

'Says who? You? Because from where I am sitting, I don't want to live the life you live.'

'Well, my awful job has paid for this extravagant five-star trip you're enjoying.' I stared at him, bewildered by yet another unthoughtful comment. There were so many things I could have said that would have crippled him, but I held back. Instead, I slowly pushed my chair back and stood up.

'My future will be the result of the decisions *I* make. Not you, Mark. I can't do this with you anymore. I'm done.' I got up from the table and walked towards the beach, hoping and praying he wouldn't follow me. He didn't. For the first time since we met, no part of me wanted to run back to him, to apologise if I had upset him, to make it work at the expense of my own wellbeing. It was there and then, alone on the beach, I made a decision to no longer take the safe road, because I knew the most uncertain one was going to be the most fulfilling for me.

Hours passed while I reflected on everything that happened during the trip – all the experiences that had slowly led me to this moment and the people who helped me discover myself. Felicity, Quella, Rod, Janine, Emily, Alice, Uncle Pat, Gary, Christian and John. It was clear that sitting behind a desk in the corporate world was no longer my future, and no longer was Mark. I could see they were safety nets I had hung onto because of conditioning. I was trying to be the perfect partner and the perfect citizen by everyone else's standards but my own.

Sitting there in the dark, listening to the waves crashing against the shore, I wondered if all along I was somehow getting these subtle hints. From the people I'd met, the dreams I'd had and the situations I found myself in. This was yet another one, another fork in the road where I had the choice to stay on the path I was on, or move in another direction. I stayed on that beach until the purging subsided and the fog lifted in my mind and somehow I could make sense of it all.

Please don't be there, Mark, I thought as I walked to our room. If it wasn't so late, I would have tried to get another. The lights were on. He was there. I knocked three times and heard loud, fast footsteps as he rushed to the door and opened it.

'That was so dangerous!' he yelled, looking worried.

'Mark, we need to talk!' I said, standing still.

'Look, I'm sorry, I was out of line doing that with Eileen.'

'I know, Mark. It was. But it's deeper than that, and you know it,' I said, looking down so he didn't have to see the tears falling from my eyes once more.

'What do you mean?' he asked. 'Become a photographer, I don't care, become one if that's what you want.'

'We met each other in university, Mark, so much has changed since then. We have grown, but in two very different directions, and not together. I've changed on this trip alone and I am not that same girl you still think I am,' I said, my voice breaking but trying my best to sit in the uncomfortable situation we were in. Mark didn't say anything this time. He knew, I was just the one brave enough to say it.

'But maybe when we go home, things will go back to normal?' he asked quietly.

'Mark, have you noticed how many times you've said "maybe when"? I can't live in maybe-whens anymore. I don't know if you realised how miserable I was in Manhattan. I stayed for you. I refuse to wait up for you at night, I refuse to work in a big grey building doing something I hate.'

The more I spoke, the more I realised how much truth I was speaking.

'That's the real world, Katelyn, no-one likes their job,' he said, getting frustrated. I didn't think anymore words could have explained to him what I meant, how limiting his belief was.

'I'm not going back to New York with you, Mark,' I finally said, quietly, but this time keeping eye contact. He rubbed his face and started gathering pillows and blankets, throwing them on the couch.

'I'll leave in the morning,' he said, the room now falling silent so we could hear the ocean outside. I went into the bathroom and turned the shower on, sitting on the floor crying as quietly as I could, my tears diluting and washing away the words and feelings of the night. I didn't want to face him again; instead I curled up on the cool tile floor, wrapped in towels, and fell asleep from pure emotional exhaustion.

37

Freedom

I woke up to the sound of laughter. I heard a group of girls passing the window of the bathroom. I lifted my head, stretching it from the uncomfortable position I fell asleep in. Standing up, I saw Mark's toothbrush and shaver, knowing he hadn't come in. I took a breath, ready to face him outside. He was gone. He had taken everything except for his toiletries. *What time did he leave? Where did he go?* I walked to the balcony still wrapped in the towels from the night before, hoping that the bright blue sky and ocean breeze would lift my spirits. It didn't. I stood there, eyes closed, breathing, listening.

'Katelyn!' I heard someone yell from below. It was John, from the bar. He was jogging down the beach, full of energy and soul. The sun's glare was strong, I had to raise my arm up to shade my eyes.

'Hi, John,' I waved.

'Want to join me?' he asked. I shook my head. 'C'mon, fresh air is good for the soul. I bet you haven't seen the view from Diamond Head either, have you?' I shook my head again. I had heard about the views. It was a clear day, and it would be good for me to release some of the energy from last night.

'Give me ten!' I yelled down. John gave me a thumbs up and I found him stretching when I met him by the walkway.

'C'mon, let's go!' he said, starting the walk at a steady pace.

'What is this, a race?' I said, already laughing in his company.

'I'm sorry, how old are you again?' he teased, not slowing his speed down at all. We laughed and joked, and I felt somewhat lighter again.

'Diamond Head is a crater? That's cool!' I said, reading the sign out the front.

'It is! Ready to head up it?' he asked, giving me just enough time to take a final sip of my water. I nodded and let him lead the way. The trail was crowded with tourists. There were times we could walk faster and overtake and times we had to slow down, which worked well for me but frustrated John. It was the last flight of stairs that were the hardest and the scariest, but they gave way to the most magnificent panoramic views of Oahu.

'*Whoooaahhh!*' is the only word I could come up with as I looked in awe. There was not a cloud in the sky. It was perfect.

'Worth it?' he asked, enjoying my reaction. John had been there numerous times before. I nodded in disbelief. We stood at the top together, admiring.

'I don't want to leave here, John, but I don't know what to do,' I finally admitted.

'Mark?' he asked, although he didn't seem surprised when I said Mark had left.

'Maybe you should ask someone if they have a job and accommodation?'

I laughed and looked at him absurdly.

'John, do you have accommodation and a job for me so I can continue living in one of the most beautiful places in the world?' I asked sarcastically.

'Why yes, actually, I do.' I didn't take him seriously but played along. 'I need someone to mind my art gallery and apartment while I go to Portugal for a week. I can train you over the next few weeks before I leave, you won't have to pay rent and I'll pay you for the hours you work.' I looked back at the view, processing what he said.

'You're joking, right?' I asked, not wanting to get my hopes up but feeling my heart beat just a little faster from excitement.

'You'd actually be doing me a favour.'

'You trust me? You don't even know me!'

'I have a good feeling about you, Katelyn. There's no pressure for you to take it, but the offer is there if you'd like it.'

'I'll take it!' I said, hugging him instinctively. We stayed there for a few more moments and then slowly made our way down in single file. This time I was ahead of John, so I led the way.

He explained to me what I needed to do to run the art gallery, how I could sell my prints, where he lived, and as he spoke, an overwhelming warm feeling engulfed me. *Am I lucky? Were these opportunities always presenting themselves but was I never open enough to see them before?* I couldn't quite believe the new chapter that was waiting ahead of me, but I was ready to embrace it. No-one could wipe the smile off my face, and for the first time, I was ready to follow it.

Acknowledgements

Reflecting back on my original acknowledgements from *Strayed Love*, it makes me so grateful to see many of the OGs I thanked are still the people I want to thank today.

A special thanks to my little sister, Erin. You have always shown up to support me in anything I do, no matter what. From book launches to art exhibitions, you've always made time for me and my wild projects. I am so grateful for you.

To my best friends – while I've been blessed with many – a special thank you to Brooke, Bec and Kiaya for being a daily dose of love. To Kat and Mary – for business talks and support and showing up with physical ways to help, which you know I always struggle to ask for. Thank you all for always showing up for me.

Thank you to those that have shaped my heart, without naming names this time around, I've been so lucky to have loved and been loved as much as I have. The memories will always stay with me.

Thank you to my publisher, Karen McDermott, for making my publishing dreams a reality and to Yasmin Walter (co-owner of KMD), who has never failed to answer any question I have about … absolutely anything (the book launch is going to be so memorable thanks to you).

Lastly, thank you to all my readers – near and far. Whether you have followed my journey since travel blogging in 2013, or whether you've just discovered me through this novel. I am grateful for your support and I hope you enjoyed the journey as much as I did. There is so much more to come!

About the Author

Sheleila is the author of original novel *Strayed Love* and children's book *The Quacking Frog*. She is also a co-author in two non-fiction anthologies, *The FIFO Wives' Tales* and *Love, Bruises & Bullsh!t*.

The FIFO Wives' Tales, creating discussion on the fly-in fly-out lifestyle, won a gold Literary Titan book award in 2022 and is a number-one Amazon bestseller.

Sheleila draws inspiration through her own experiences – travelling to thirty-two countries at the time of publishing (including Iceland, England, Scotland and Hawaii). She has backpacked her way through Asia and Europe, couch-surfed from Scotland to England while touring on a $300 (£150 pound) second-hand bicycle and also reconnected with estranged family while living in Canada.

A world traveller, people lover and experience seeker – it's her mission to inspire people to move past their comfort zone.

Keep an eye out for the sequel to *Dancing Skies and City Lights,* to be released in 2024.

'You can choose courage or you can choose comfort. You cannot have both.' – Brené Brown

www.sheleila.com.au

@sheleiladp.author
Sheleila D'Pava - Author
Sheleila D'Pava